Delicacy

Delicacy

David Foenkinos

TRANSLATED FROM THE FRENCH

by Bruce Benderson

HARPER PERENNIAL

NEW YORK • LONDON • TORONTO • SYDNEY • NEW DELHI • AUCKLAND

HARPER PERENNIAL

Originally published in France under the title *La délicatesse* in 2009 by Editions Gallimard.

HarperCollins books may be purchased for educational, business, or sales promotional use. For information please write: Special Markets Department, HarperCollins Publishers, 10 East 53rd Street, New York, NY 10022.

FIRST EDITION

Designed by Betty Lew

Library of Congress Cataloging-in-Publication Data is available upon request.

ISBN 978-0-06-200436-9

11 12 13 14 15   OV/RRD   10 9 8 7 6 5 4 3 2 1

I don't know how to make peace with things,
were each moment to tear itself away from
time to give me a kiss.

CIORAN

One

Natalie was rather private (a kind of Swiss femininity). She'd gone through adolescence without trauma, and she respected crosswalks. At twenty, she saw the future as a promise. She liked to laugh, read: two pastimes that weren't often simultaneous because she preferred sad stories. Since a literary bent wasn't concrete enough for her taste, she'd decided to study economics. Under her dreamer's demeanor, there wasn't much room for "kind-of's." With a strange smile on her face, she spent hours studying curves that showed fluctuations in Estonia's gross domestic product. When adulthood approached, she occasionally happened to go back in her mind to her childhood. Instants of happiness condensed into a few episodes—always the same ones. Running on the beach, boarding an airplane, sleeping in her father's arms. But she never ever felt nostalgia. That was something that was quite rare for Natalie.*

---

* There's often a clear tendency for nostalgia in Natalies.

1

Two

❖ ❖ ❖

Most couples love to tell each other their stories and assume their meeting had something exceptional about it; countless pairings formed under the most banal conditions are, all the same, spiced up with details that produce a minor thrill. In the end, they try to analyze everything.

Natalie and François met on the street. It's always a tricky thing when a man comes up to a woman. She's bound to wonder, Is that what he spends his time doing? Quite often the men are going to claim that it's the first time. To listen to them, they are suddenly struck by a unique charm that gives them permission to brave their customary shyness. The women automatically answer that they don't have the time. Natalie wasn't breaking that rule. It was idiotic: she didn't have much to do and liked the idea of being approached like that. No one had ever dared. Several times she'd asked herself, Do I seem too sullen, too lethargic? One of her friends had told her: nobody ever stops you because you have the look of a woman hounded by passing time.

———

When a man comes up to a woman he doesn't know, he's supposed to say lovely things. Could there ever be a male kamikaze who'd stop a woman and fling at her, "How can you be wearing those shoes? Your toes look like they're in a gulag. It's shameful, you're Stalin when it comes to your feet!" Who would say such a thing? Certainly not François, who'd wisely settled on the complimentary approach. He tried to define the least definable thing that exists: confusion. Why had he stopped her? It had mostly to do with the way she walked. He'd sensed something new, almost childlike, like a rhapsody of kneecaps. She emanated a kind of touchingly natural manner, a grace of movement, and he thought, She's exactly the kind of woman I'd like to go with me to Geneva for the weekend. So he took himself firmly in hand (both hands, though at that moment he wished he had four). Especially because this really was the first time for him. Right then and right there on this sidewalk, they were meeting. An absolutely classical beginning, which is often how things that end up less so start.

He stammered the first few words, when suddenly all of it came pouring out, crystal clear. A somewhat pathetic and desperate, yet terribly touching, energy took control. Therein lies the magic of our paradoxes: the situation was so uncomfortable that he pulled through with elegance. By the end of thirty seconds he'd even managed to make her smile. This created a breach in the anonymity. She agreed to have coffee, and he understood that she wasn't in the slightest hurry. He found it amazing to be able to spend a moment like this with a woman who'd just entered his field of vision. He'd always liked to watch women in the street. He even remembered having been kind of a romantic teenager who was capable of following girls from good families right up to the door of their apartments. He'd even changed cars in the subway to get near a passenger he'd spotted from a distance. Although prey to the dictates of physical desire, he remained no less a romantic man, believing that the realm of women could be shrunk to one woman.

So he asked her what she'd like to drink. Her choice would be crucial. If she orders a decaf, he thought, I'm getting up and leaving. No one was entitled to drink a decaf when it came to this type of encounter. It's the least gregarious drink there is. Tea isn't much better. Just met, and already settling into some kind of dull cocoon. You feel like you're going to end up spending Sunday afternoons watching TV. Or worse: at the in-laws'. Yes, tea is indisputably in-law territory. Then what? Alcohol? No good for this time of day. You could have qualms about a woman who starts drinking right away like that. Even a glass of red wine isn't going to cut it. François kept waiting for her to choose what she'd like to drink, and this was how he kept up his liquid analysis of first impressions of women. What was left now? Coke, or any type of soda . . . no, not possible, that didn't say woman at all. Might as well ask for a straw, too, while she was at it. Finally he decided that juice was good. Yes, juice, that was nice. It's friendly and not too aggressive. You can sense the kind of sweet, well-balanced woman who would make such a choice. But which juice? Better to avoid the great classics: apple, orange, too popular. It would have to be only slightly original without being completely eccentric. Papaya or guava—frightening. No, the best is choosing something in between, like apricot. That's it. Apricot juice: perfect. If she chooses it, I'll marry her, thought François. At that precise instant, Natalie raised her head from the menu, as if emerging from a long reflection. It was the same reflection in which the stranger opposite her had just been absorbed.

"I'll have a juice . . ."

" . . . ?"

"Apricot juice, I guess."

He looked at her as if she were a violation of reality.

Her reason for agreeing to sit down with a stranger was that she'd fallen under his charm. She'd immediately liked his mixture of awkwardness and obviousness, an attitude floundering between Pierre Richard and Marlon Brando. Physically, he had something she appreciated in men: he was a little cross-eyed. Just a little, but still enough to notice. Yes, finding this detail about him was incredible. What's more, he was called François. She'd always liked that name. Elegant and calm—like her idea of the fifties. He spoke more and more effortlessly now. No more lapses in the conversation, no more embarrassment, tension. Ten minutes later, that first incursion in the street had been forgotten. They felt like they'd already met, were seeing each other because they had a date. The simplicity of it was disconcerting: a simplicity that made all the other dates they'd had before baffling, those times they'd had to talk or try to be amusing, make an effort to seem like a worthwhile person. The obviousness of it became almost laughable. Natalie gazed at this no-longer-strange boy while each particle of anonymity progressively dissolved right before her eyes. She tried to remember where she'd been going when she met him. It was a blur. She wasn't the type to go walking for no reason. Hadn't she wanted to walk in the traces of that Cortázar novel she'd just read? Now, between them, there was literature. Yes, that was it, she'd read *Hopscotch* and had particularly liked those scenes where hero and heroine try to run into each other in the street, although they're following *routes born of a clochard phrase.** In the evening, they reconstructed their itineraries on a map, to see at what moment they could have met, at what moments they were bound to have brushed by each other. So that's where she was headed: into a novel.

---

* Translator's note: from *Hopscotch* (original Spanish title: *Rayuela*), translated from the Spanish by Gregory Rabassa. Copyright © 1966 by Random House, Inc.

Three

Natalie's Three Favorite Novels

Her Lover by Albert Cohen

*

The Lover by Marguerite Duras

*

Separation by Dan Franck

Four

❖ ❖ ❖

François worked in finance. Five minutes with him was enough to reveal this to be as incongruous as Natalie's career in marketing. Maybe there's a tyranny of the concrete that permanently frustrates careers. That said, it's difficult to imagine what else he could have done. We may have experienced him as almost timid when he was meeting Natalie, but this was a man who was full of vitality, bursting with ideas and energy. He was enthusiastic enough to tackle any profession—even sales rep with tie. He was a man you'd have no trouble imagining with a briefcase, squeezing hands while hoping to squeeze necks. He had that annoying charm of somebody who can sell you anything at all. You'd go skiing with him in the summer and swimming with him in a lake in Iceland. He was the kind of man who'd approach a woman in the street just once and end up with the right one. For him, everything seemed to work. So, finance—why not? He belonged to that group of novice traders who gambled with millions and remembered not so long ago Monopoly games. But as soon as he was away from his bank, he became another man. He left the Standard & Poor's where it belonged. His profession hadn't kept him from his enthusiasms. Most of all, he liked puz-

zles. That may seem strange, but nothing channeled his intensity more than spending certain Saturdays putting together thousands of pieces. Natalie enjoyed watching her fiancé crouched in the living room. A silent spectacle. Suddenly, he'd stand up and shout, "Come on, we're going out!" That's the last thing that should be pointed out about him. He was no fan of transitions. He liked disruptions, passing from silence to bursts of activity.

With François, time flew—at a frenzied pace. You'd have believed he could skip days, create strange weeks that had no Thursday. They'd barely met and were already celebrating two years together. Two years without the slightest blemish, enough to baffle any plate-smasher. You watched them the way you'd admire a champion. They were gold medalists of love. Natalie brilliantly pursued her studies, all the while adding ease to François's daily life. Choosing a man who was just a little bit older than she and who already had a professional position had allowed her to leave her family. But not wanting to depend upon him for financial survival, she'd decided to work a few evenings a week in the theater as an usherette. She enjoyed a job that offset the rather austere atmosphere of the university. Once the audience had been seated, she went to her place at the back. She'd sit down and watch a show she knew by heart. She moved her lips in sync with the actresses and smiled with gracious appreciation while the audience was applauding. Then she sold them the program.

Knowing the plays perfectly, she enjoyed embellishing her daily portion of dialogues, striding up and down the living room while yowling that the cat was dead. These last few evenings, she was playing Musset's *Lorenzaccio*, tossing out a random series of lines now and then with perfect incoherence. "Come here, the Hungarian is right." Or else: "Who is that in the mud? Who grovels before the walls of my palace with such horrible screams?" This is what François was being treated to that day, while he tried to concentrate. "Can you make a little less noise?" he asked.

"Yes, sure."

"I'm doing a really major puzzle."

So Natalie quieted down, out of respect for her boyfriend's dedication. This puzzle seemed different from the others. You couldn't see any patterns, any castles or characters. It was composed of red loops on a white background. Loops that were turning into letters. It was a message in the form of a puzzle. Natalie let go of the book she'd just opened to watch the puzzle taking shape. Occasionally François turned around to look at her. The process of discovery continued toward its conclusion. There were only a few pieces left; Natalie could already guess the message, a painstakingly created one, made of hundreds of pieces. Yes, now she could read what it said: "Do you want to become my wife?"

Five

❖ ❖ ❖

*Top Scorers of the World of Puzzles Championship
in Minsk, October 27 to November 1, 2008*

1. Ulrich Voigt (Germany): 1,464 points
2. Mehmet Murat Sevim (Turkey): 1,266 points
3. Roger Barkan (United States): 1,241 points

Six

❖ ❖ ❖

To keep such an impeccable routine from being thwarted, the wedding was wonderfully executed. A celebration that was simple and sweet, neither gaudy nor too serious. There was a bottle of champagne for every guest; that was practical. The good humor was genuine. You have to be merry for a wedding. Much more so than for a birthday. There's a hierarchy of responsibilities for joyousness, and marriage sits at the top of the pyramid. You should smile and dance and, later, pressure the old people to go to bed. Let us not forget the beauty of Natalie, who'd worked on her appearance with mounting application, tending to her weight and her looks for weeks. A perfectly mastered work of preparation: she was at the height of her beauty. Such a singular moment had to be fixed in time, just as Armstrong had planted the American flag on the moon. François studied her with emotion and fixed the moment in his memory better than anyone else. Before him stood his wife, and he knew this image was the one that would pass before his eyes at his moment of death. It came down to perfect happiness. Then she stood up, took hold of the microphone, and sang a Beatles song.* François

---

* "Here, There and Everywhere" (1966).

was crazy for John Lennon. He was, in fact, wearing white to pay homage to him. And so, when the newlyweds danced, the whiteness of one was lost in the whiteness of the other.

Unfortunately, it began raining. This prevented the guests from taking a little air outside, under the heavens, and contemplating the stars that had been rented for the occasion. In such cases, people love to come up with ridiculous sayings, such as, "Rainy wedding, happy marriage." Why are we constantly subjected to such absurd utterances? Of course, they weren't being serious. It was raining and just a bit sad, that's all. The party was less lavish cut off from these breathing sessions in the open air. You'd get stifled fast watching the rain fall harder and harder. Some would leave sooner than planned. Others would keep dancing in the same way they would have if it had snowed. Still others would think twice. Was this really important for the wedding couple?

Comes that hour of happiness when you're alone in the crowd. Yes, they were alone in the whirl of melodies and waltzes. We have to twirl as long as possible, he was saying, twirl to the point of no longer knowing where to go. She stopped thinking of everything. For the first time, life was lived in its unique, all-embracing density: the present.

François took Natalie by the waist and led her outside. They ran through the garden. She said to him, "You're crazy," but it was a craziness that made her mad with joy. Now they were drenched, hidden by the trees. In the night, under the rain, they lay on bare ground, which was becoming muddy. The whiteness of their clothing was only a memory. François took off his wife's dress, accepting that it was what he'd wanted to do since the start of the evening. He could even have done it at church. An instant way of honoring the two "I do's." But he'd held back his desire until this moment. Natalie was surprised by his intensity. She'd already stopped thinking a moment ago. She took cues from her husband, trying to breathe correctly, trying not to get carried away by all this ravaging. Her desire obeyed François's. She had such longing to be taken by him now, on their first night as husband and wife. She was waiting, waiting, and François was talking his head off, François was in the throes of an insane energy, an outrageous appetite for pleasure. Except that, just as he penetrated her, he felt paralyzed. An anxiety that may have been related to fear of joy too intense; but no, it was something else, another thing holding him back at that instant. And keeping him from going on. "What's happening?" she asked him. And he answered, "Nothing . . . nothing . . . it's just the first time I've made love with a married woman."

Seven

❖ ❖ ❖

Examples of Ridiculous Sayings People Love to Repeat

One lost, ten found.

*

To live happy, live hidden.

*

A laughing woman is halfway to bed.

Eight

✦ ✦ ✦

They'd been on a honeymoon, they'd taken photos, and they'd come back. Now it was time to start real life. Natalie had finished school more than six months ago. Up until now, she'd used the alibi of getting ready for the wedding to keep from looking for work. Organizing a marriage is like forming a government after a war. And what should be done with collaborators? Justifying all the time put into it is so complicated. Well, that wasn't altogether true. More than anything, she'd wanted to spend some time on herself, time to read, hang out, as if she'd known she wasn't going to get such times later. That she'd be snatched up by professional life and, of course, her life as a wife.

It was time to go to interviews. After a few tries, she realized it wasn't that easy. So this was normal life? But she thought she'd landed a degree that was recognized, and gained experience through several important internships that hadn't been confined to serving coffee between two Xerox sessions. She had an appointment for a job interview at a Swedish company. She was surprised to be welcomed directly by the boss, instead of the director of human resources. When it came to recruitment, he wanted full control. That was his official version of the facts. The truth was much more pragmatic: he'd stopped by the department of human resources and seen Natalie's photo on her CV. It was a strange enough photo; you couldn't really assess her body. Of course, you suspected she wasn't devoid of beauty, but this wasn't what had attracted the boss's eye. It was something else. Something he couldn't seem to define but had a feeling about: good sense. Yes, that's what he'd suspected. He thought this woman seemed sensible.

Charles Delamain wasn't Swedish. But you need only enter his office to wonder whether he harbored an ambition to be, no doubt to please his shareholders. On a piece of Ikea furniture could be seen a plate with several small biscuits that make a lot of crumbs.

"I thought your career path was very interesting . . . and . . ."

"Yes?"

"You're wearing a wedding ring. Are you married?"

"Uh . . . yes."

There was a pause in the conversation. Charles had looked at the young woman's CV a number of times, and he hadn't seen that she was married. The moment she said "yes," he took another look at the CV. So, she was married. It was as if, in his brain, the photo had scrambled the young woman's personal status. But was it really so important? He had to keep the interview going to keep the slightest discomfort from building.

"And are you planning on having children?" he continued.

"Not for the moment," Natalie answered, without the slightest hesitation.

Such a question could seem completely normal during an interview with a young woman who'd just gotten married. But she sensed something different, without really being able to define it. Charles had stopped talking and was looking hard at her. Finally, he got up and took a biscuit.

"Would you like a Krisprolls?"

"No thanks."

"You ought to."

"Nice of you, but I'm not hungry."

"You ought to get used to it. That's all we eat here."

"You mean . . . that . . . ?"

"Yes."

Nine

Sometimes Natalie had the impression that people were jealous of her happiness. It was a vague feeling, nothing really concrete, just a passing hunch. But she felt it. Through details, smiles that barely registered but spoke volumes, ways of looking at her. No one could imagine that she sometimes was afraid of this happiness, afraid that it could contain the threat of unhappiness. Sometimes she stopped herself when she found herself saying, "I'm happy," a sort of superstition, a sort of memory of all those moments when life had finally veered onto the wrong track.

Her family and the friends who'd come to the wedding formed what could be called the *first circle of social pressure*. Pressure to have a child. Could it be that they were sick enough at this point of their own lives to get worked up about those of others? That's always the case. We live under the dictates of others' desires. Natalie and François didn't want to become a TV series for their crowd. For the moment, they loved the idea of being two people alone in the world, in the most perfect cliché of romantic schmaltzy serenity. Since they'd met, they'd been living in a momentum of absolute freedom. Adoring travel, taking advantage of the slightest sunny weekend, they'd gone all over Europe with the innocence of romance. There was evidence of their love in Rome, Lisbon, or even Berlin. More than ever, spreading themselves thin gave them the feeling of being one. These trips also brought them a real sense of a storybook life. They were crazy about evenings during which they'd again tell the story of how they met, recalling the details with pleasure, glorying in the accuracy of chance. When it came to the mythology of their love, they were like children tirelessly interested in hearing the same story.

So, yes, such happiness could inspire fear.

Day-to-day life hadn't worn them down. Both were working more and more, so they made sure to connect. Lunch together, even a quick one. Lunching "on a dime," François would call it. And Natalie loved that expression. She'd imagine a contemporary painting showing a couple lunching on a dime, as in a picnic on the grass. That was a painting Dalí could have done, she'd say. Sometimes there are turns of phrase we adore, that we find delightful, whereas the person who said them doesn't realize it. François liked the idea of a Dalí painting, liked the fact that his wife could invent, and even modify, the story of the painting. It was a form of naïveté pushed to the max. He whispered that he wanted her now, wanted to carry her off somewhere and take her, anywhere at all. Couldn't, she had to leave. So he'd wait until evening and throw himself on her with the accumulated desire of the frustrated hours he'd passed. Time didn't seem to dull their sex life. Something rare: every day together still had traces of their first day.

———

They also tried to keep up a social life, continue to see friends, go to the theater, and make surprise visits to their grandparents. They tried not to let themselves get isolated. To avoid the trap of losing enthusiasm. Years went by in this way, and everything seemed so simple. Whereas others had to work at it. Natalie didn't understand the expression "Being in a relationship takes work." As she saw it, things were simple or they weren't. It's quite easy to think such a thing when everything is on the level, when no one makes waves. Although there were some, at times. But that made you wonder if they argued only for the pleasure of making up. Come on, really? So much success was becoming disturbing. Time went by with such fluency, on that rare talent of being alive.

Ten

✦ ✦ ✦

Natalie and François's Future Travel Plans

Barcelona

*

Miami

*

La Baule

Eleven

❖ ❖ ❖

Just breathe, and time will pass. It was already five years since
Natalie had started working for her Swedish company. Five years
of all types of work, going back and forth in the hallways and in
and out of the elevator. Not far from the equivalent of a Paris–
Moscow trip. Five years and 1,212 coffees drunk from the machine, 324 of which were drunk during four hundred meetings
with clients. Charles was very happy about counting her among
his close collaborators. It wasn't unusual for him to call her into
his office just to congratulate her. Certainly by preference he
tended to do it in the evening. When everyone had left. But not in
a crude way. He felt a lot of affection for her and valued those moments when they found themselves alone. Of course, he was trying to create a context favorable to ambiguity. No other woman
would have been duped by such a ploy, but Natalie was living in
the peculiar ether of monogamy. Sorry: of love. The love that
annihilates all other men, but also any objectivity about seduction attempts. Charles had fun with it and thought of this François as a myth. Perhaps her way of never existing in a context of
seduction also seemed like a kind of challenge to him. One day
or another, he'd inevitably manage to create a dubious context

between them, be it minimal. Sometimes he changed his attitude radically and regretted having hired her. Gazing at that inaccessible womanliness day after day was draining for him.

Natalie's relationship with her boss, which the others saw as privileged, created tensions. She tried to allay them, to keep away from the petty intrigues of office life. If she kept her distance with Charles, it was also for that reason. To avoid slipping into the old-fashioned role of favorite. Her gracefulness and the aura she created around her boss probably made it even more necessary. That's what she resented, without knowing if it was justified. Everyone agreed that this brilliant, energetic, hardworking young woman was bound to have a great future with the company. On several occasions, the Swedish stockholders got wind of her excellent initiatives. The jealousies she aroused materialized in low blows. Attempts to undermine her. She wouldn't complain, was never the type to moan when she came back to François in the evening. It was also a way of saying that the freak show of one-upmanship had no more importance than just that. Such a capacity for letting problems glance off her passed for strength. This was perhaps her most attractive talent: not letting her weaknesses show.

Twelve

Distance from Paris to Moscow

1,540 miles

Thirteen

❖ ❖ ❖

Natalie was often exhausted on weekends. On Sunday, she liked to lie on the couch and read, trying to alternate between pages and dreams when drowsiness got the better of fiction. She put a blanket over her legs. And what else? Oh, yes, she liked to make tea, of which she drank several cups, by small sips, as if the tea were a never-ending spring. The Sunday when everything happened, she was reading a long Russian tale by a writer who's less read than Tolstoy or Dostoevsky and can make you think about the injustice of posterity. She liked the hero's spinelessness, his inability to react, to imprint daily life with his energy. There was a sadness in that weakness. She liked romans-fleuves the way she liked her tea.

François came up to her. "What are you reading?" She said it was a Russian author, but she wasn't more specific because he seemed to have asked the question only out of politeness, mechanically. It was Sunday. She liked to read, he to run. He was wearing those shorts she thought looked a bit ridiculous. She couldn't have known that she was seeing them for the last time. He was hopping all over the place. He had that way of always wanting to do his warm-up in their living room, working himself up to breathing hard before going out, as if he wanted to leave a big emptiness behind him. He'd succeed at it, that was sure. Before going out, he bent toward his wife and said something to her. Strangely, she wouldn't remember these words. Their last exchange would vanish into thin air. And then she fell asleep.

When she awoke, it was difficult to know how long she'd been dozing. Ten minutes or an hour? She served herself a little more tea. It was still warm. That was some indication. Nothing seemed to have changed. It was exactly the same situation as before she'd fallen asleep. Yes, everything was identical. The telephone rang during this return to the identical. The sound of the ring mixed with the steam from the tea, in a strange synchronization of sensations. Natalie answered. A second later, her life was no longer the same. She instinctively put a bookmark in her book and rushed outdoors.

When she got to the hospital lobby, she didn't know what to say, what to do. She stayed there without moving for a long moment. At reception, she was finally told where to find her husband, and she found him on his back. Perfectly still. She thought, It looks as though he's sleeping. He never moves at night. And for that particular instant it was just like any other night.

"What are the chances?" Natalie asked the doctor.

"Negligible."

"What does negligible mean? Is negligible none? If that's the case, tell me it's none."

"I can't say, ma'am. The chance is minuscule. You never know."

"But you do, you ought to know! It's your job to know!"

She'd shouted that sentence with all her strength. Several times. Then she'd stopped. She'd looked hard at the doctor, and he, too, was absolutely still, paralyzed. He'd witnessed a lot of dramatic scenes. But without being able to explain why, he experienced this one as one degree higher in the hierarchy of tragedies. He contemplated this woman's face, contorted by grief. Unable to cry because the pain had drained away everything. She came toward him, ruined, vacant. Before collapsing.

When she came to, she saw her parents. As well as François's. A moment before, she'd been reading, and suddenly she wasn't home anymore. Reality pieced itself together again. She wanted to travel backward into sleep, backward into that Sunday. It can't be. It can't be, was what she kept repeating in a delirious litany. They explained to her that he was in a coma. That nothing had been lost, but she sensed quite clearly that everything was over. She knew it. She didn't feel like fighting. For what? To keep a life going for a week. And after? She'd seen him. She'd seen his stillness. You don't come back from that kind of stillness. You stay that way forever.

They gave her tranquilizers. Everything and everybody in the world around her had collapsed. And she was supposed to speak. Cheer up. It was beyond her.

"I'm going to stay with him. Watch over him."

"No, there's no reason for it. It's better for you to go home and rest a bit," said her mother.

"I don't want to rest. I have to stay here, I have to."

As she said it, she was about to faint. The doctor tried to convince her to go with her parents. She asked, "But what if he wakes up and I'm not here?" There was a pained silence. No one believed he would. They tried to reassure her, but they were kidding themselves. "We'll let you know immediately, but right now it's really better for you to get some rest." Natalie didn't answer. Everyone was pressuring her to lie down, to give in to the pull of gravity. So she left with her parents. Her mother made some bouillon that she couldn't swallow. She took two more tablets and fell into bed. In her bedroom, the one from her childhood. This morning she'd still been a woman. And now she was sleeping like a little girl.

Fourteen

❖ ❖ ❖

Possible Sentences Spoken by François Before He Went Running

I love you.

✳

I adore you.

✳

Sports first, relax later.

✳

What are we having to eat tonight?

✳

Enjoy your reading, darling.

✳

Can't wait to get back to you.

✳

I'm not planning on getting run over.

✳

We really need to invite Bernard and Nicole to dinner.

✳

You know, I should read a book, too.

*

I'm going to work really hard on my calves today.

*

Tonight we're making a baby.

Fifteen

❖ ❖ ❖

A few days later, he was dead. Natalie was in a daze, knocked out by tranquilizers. She kept thinking of their last moment together. It was too ridiculous. How could all that happiness be shattered in such a way? End with the absurd sight of a man hopping around a living room. And then those last words spoken into her ear. She'd never remember them. Maybe he'd just given her a little puff of air on the neck. He had to have been a ghost already, the moment he left. In human form, certainly, but able to create only silence, because death had already settled in.

The day of the funeral, everybody was there. They all met where François had spent his childhood. Such a crowd of people would have made him happy, she thought. But then, they wouldn't, since it was ridiculous to think about that kind of thing. How can a dead person be happy about anything? He's decomposing in a box made of four wooden planks: happy? As she walked behind the casket surrounded by close relations, another thought occurred to her: they were the same guests who were at her wedding. Yes, all of them were here. Exactly the same. A few years later, we meet again, and some of them are definitely dressed the same. Dusted off their only dark suit, suitable for good fortune as much as for misfortune. Only difference: the weather. Today was beautiful, you almost felt too warm. A high point for the month of February. Yes, the sun goes on and on. And Natalie, looking straight at it, almost burned her eyes doing so, blurred her vision in a halo of cold light.

They put him in the ground, and that was it.

After the funeral, Natalie's only wish was to be alone. She didn't want to go back to her parents'. She was tired of the pitying looks they gave her. She wanted to lie low, lock herself in, live in a tomb. Friends rode back with her. During the entire car trip, nobody knew what to say. The driver suggested a little music. But very quickly, Natalie asked him to turn it off. It was unbearable. Every song reminded her of François. Every note echoed a memory, an anecdote, a laugh. She realized how horrible it was going to be. In the seven years they'd lived together, he'd had time to leave traces of himself everywhere, on every breath. She understood that there was nothing she could experience that could make her forget his death.

Her friends helped her bring up her belongings. But she wouldn't let them come in with her.

"I won't ask you to stay, I'm tired."

"Promise to call if you need anything?"

"I will."

"Promise?"

"Yes, I promise."

———

She hugged, kissed, and thanked them. What a relief to be alone. Other people wouldn't have been able to stand being alone at that moment. Natalie had yearned for it. And yet, these circumstances added more of the unbearable to the unbearable. She walked into their living room, and everything was there. To the smallest detail. Nothing had moved. The blanket, still on the couch. The teapot, on the low table, as well, holding the book she'd been reading. She was struck by the sight of the bookmark, especially. The book was cut in two by it: the first part, read while François was alive. And at page 321, he was dead. What should she do? Can you keep reading a book interrupted by the death of your husband?

Sixteen

No one understands people who say they want to be alone. Desiring solitude is bound to be a morbid impulse. No matter how much Natalie tried to put everyone's mind at rest, they wanted to come and see her. Which amounted to obliging her to speak. Although she didn't know what to say. She was under the impression that she was going to have to go back and start again at zero, even relearn language. Maybe in the end all of them had been right to force her to socialize a bit, to force her to wash, dress, entertain. Her entourage took turns, which was horribly clear. It made her think of a sort of emergency-crisis committee, managing tragedy with the help of a secretary—her mother, obviously—who kept track of everything on a giant calendar in a way that adeptly varied family visits with visits from friends. She heard the members of the support group talking to each other, commenting on her slightest actions. "So, how's she doing?" "What's she doing?" "What's she eating?" She had the impression of suddenly having become the center of the world, whereas her world no longer existed.

Charles was the most frequent of the visitors. He stopped over every two or three days. According to him this was also a way of *keeping her in contact with the professional milieu*. He talked to her about the developmental reports in progress, and she looked at him like a lunatic. What in hell's name could it matter to her whether Chinese foreign trade was undergoing a crisis at the moment? Were the Chinese going to bring back her husband? No. Fine. Then it was useless. Charles was perfectly aware that she wasn't listening to him, but he knew that it would gradually have an effect. That he was filtering in elements of reality drop by drop, like an infusion. That China, and even Sweden, were reconstituting Natalie's horizon. Charles would sit down very close to her.

"You can start again when you feel like it. You should know that the entire company's behind you."

"Thank you, how nice."

"And you know that you can count on me."

"Thanks."

"*Really* count on me."

She didn't understand why he'd begun using the informal form of the French word for *you* with her since her husband's death. What was the real meaning of it? But why look for meaning in this abrupt change? She didn't have the strength to. Maybe he felt some responsibility to show her that an entire side of her life was stable. But even so, his addressing her in this familiar way felt strange. But then, it didn't really; there are certain things you can't say using the formal word for *you*. Comforting things. You had to eliminate the distance to say them, had to get personal. He was stopping by a little too often, it occurred to her. She tried to make him understand that. But people who are crying aren't listened to. He kept being there, and he was becoming insistent. One evening, while talking to her, he put his hand on her knee. She said nothing, but she thought he had a woeful lack of sensitivity. Did he want to take advantage of her grief and try to take François's place? Was he the type to play second fiddle in this requiem? Maybe he had simply wanted her to understand that if she needed affection, he was there. Should she have a need to make love. It isn't unusual for nearness to death to push you into the sexual realm. But in this case, not really. It was impossible for her to imagine another man. So she pushed away Charles's hand, and he must have felt he'd gone too far.

"I'll come back to work soon," she said.

Without really knowing what this "soon" meant.

Seventeen

❖ ❖ ❖

Why Roman Polanski Adapted
Thomas Hardy's Novel
Tess of the d'Urbervilles *for the Screen*

This isn't exactly like having your reading of a book interrupted by death. But Roman Polanski's wife, Sharon Tate, before being savagely murdered by followers of Charles Manson, had pointed out this book to her husband and told him it was ideal for an adaptation. The film, made around ten years later and starring Natassja Kinski, was therefore dedicated to her.

Eighteen

Natalie and François hadn't wanted a child right away. It was a plan for the future, a future that didn't exist anymore. Their child would remain a virtual one. Sometimes you think about all those artists who died and wonder what their creations would have been like if they'd survived. What would John Lennon have composed in 1992 if he hadn't died in 1980? Likewise: what would the life of that child who would never exist have been like? You'd have to think about all those fates that foundered on the banks of their potential.

For weeks, her point of view had come close to insanity: denying death. Imagining everyday life as if her husband were still there. She was capable of leaving notes for him on the living room table before going out for a walk in the morning. She'd walk for hours, with only one desire: to lose herself in the crowd. Sometimes she also went into churches, despite the fact that she wasn't a believer. And was convinced she never would be. She had trouble understanding people taking refuge in religion, trouble understanding that you could have faith after having lived through tragedy. However, sitting there in the middle of the afternoon, surrounded by empty pews, she was comforted by the place. It was just a shred of relief, but for a split second, yes, she felt the warmth of Christ. Then she got onto her knees, and she was like a saint with the devil in her heart.

Sometimes she went back to the place they'd met. To that sidewalk on which she'd walked, unknown to him, seven years before. She wondered, "And if someone else approached me now, how would I react?" But no one came to interrupt her meditation.

She also went to the place where her husband had been run over. Where, jogging, in his shorts, with music in his ears, he'd blundered across the street. Made the ultimate blunder. She would stand on the curb and watch the cars go by. Why not kill herself at the same spot? Why not blend the traces of their blood in a final, morbid union. She'd stay a long time without knowing what to do, tears trickling down her face. Especially in the days following the funeral, she came back to this place. She didn't know why she needed to hurt herself so badly. Being there was ridiculous, imagining the brutality of impact was ridiculous, wanting to make the death of her husband concrete in this way was ridiculous. Perhaps, deep down, it was simply the only solution? Does anyone know what to do next after such a tragedy? There aren't any instructions. All of us read what's written by our bodies. Natalie was giving in to an urge to be there, to weep at the curb, to drown in her tears.

Nineteen

❈　❈　❈

John Lennon's Discography If He Hadn't Died in 1980

Still Yoko (1982)

✳

Yesterday and Tomorrow (1987)

✳

Berlin (1990)

✳

Titanic: The Soundtrack (1997)

✳

The Beatles: A Revival (1999)

Twenty

❖ ❖ ❖

The Life of Charlotte Baron
Since the Day She Ran Over François

If it hadn't been for the September 11, 2001, terrorist attacks, Charlotte Baron certainly never would have become a florist. September 11 was her birthday. Her father, who was traveling in China, had sent her flowers. Jean-Michel was climbing the stairs, not yet knowing that the times had just been turned upside down. He rang and discovered Charlotte's pallid face. She couldn't pronounce a single word. Taking the flowers, she asked, "You heard?"

"What?"

"Come . . ."

Jean-Michel and Charlotte spent the day together on the couch, watching replays of the planes crashing into the towers. Living such a moment together created a powerful bond. They became inseparable, even had an affair for several months before concluding they were more friends than lovers.

———

Somewhat later, Jean-Michel started his own flower delivery
company and asked Charlotte to work with him. From then on,
their life was about making bouquets. The Sunday the accident
happened, Jean-Michel had prepared everything. The customer
wanted to ask his girlfriend to marry him. When she received
flowers, she'd get the message; it was a kind of coded signal between the two. Having the flowers delivered that Sunday was
crucial, because it was the anniversary of their meeting. Just before leaving, Jean-Michel got a call from his mother: his grandfather had just been hospitalized. Charlotte said she'd take care
of the delivery. She liked to drive the van a lot. Especially when
there was only one stop to make and there was no hurry. She
was thinking of the couple and the role she was playing in their
story: a secret factor. She was thinking about all of this, as well
as other things, when a man crossed the street haphazardly. And
she hit the brakes too late.

Charlotte was devastated by the accident. A psychologist tried
to make her talk about it, to make sure she recovered from the
shock as soon as possible, so the trauma wouldn't eat away at
her unconscious. Quickly enough, she wondered, Should I get
in touch with the widow? She finally decided that it wouldn't
do any good. At any rate, what could she have said? "I'm sorry."
Do you apologize in such cases? Maybe she would have added,
"It was stupid of your husband to run like that, without car-
ing how; he's screwing up my life, too, are you aware of that?
You think it's easy to go on living when you've killed somebody?" Sometimes she had genuine outbursts of hate for that

man, for his thoughtlessness. But most of the time she kept quiet. She sat around in a state of blankness. The periods of silence linked her to Natalie. Both of them were floating in the anesthesia of a path of least resistance. For weeks during her recovery, without knowing why, she thought constantly of the flowers she was supposed to deliver on the day of the accident. The bouquet that never made it stood for time come to nothing. Incessantly, the event replayed in slow motion right before her eyes, including the sound of the impact, over and over. The flowers were always there in the foreground, blurring her view. They shrouded her day and became her obsession in petal form.

Jean-Michel, very worried about her state of mind, worked himself into a lather trying to get her to go back to work. It was one attempt to rouse her that was as good as any other. And it worked, since she lifted her head and answered yes, like little girls sometimes do when promising to be good after having done something stupid. Deep down, she knew very well that she had no other choice. She had to go on. And it certainly wasn't the sudden incitement coming from her colleague that talked her into it. Everything will go back to the way it was, thought Charlotte, her mind at ease. But no, nothing could go back to the way it was. Something had brutally shattered in the progression of days. That Sunday was there forever: you would find it on Monday and on Thursday. And it kept alive on Friday or Tuesday. That Sunday was never settled and began to look like goddamn eternity; it spread itself all over the future. Charlotte was smiling, Charlotte was eating, but a dark cloud covered Charlotte's face. She seemed obsessed with a single idea. Suddenly, she asked, "Those flowers I was supposed to deliver that day . . . did you ever deliver them?"

"I had other things on my mind. I went to find you right away."

"But the man didn't call?"

"Yes, of course. I talked to him on the phone the next day. He wasn't happy about it at all. His girlfriend didn't get anything."

"And then?"

"And then . . . I explained it to him . . . I told him you'd had an accident . . . that a man was in a coma . . ."

"And what did he say?"

"I don't remember very well anymore . . . he apologized . . . and then he muttered something . . . I think he saw it as some kind of sign. Something very negative."

"You mean . . . you think he didn't ask the girl to marry him?"

"I don't know."

Charlotte was disturbed by that story. She took the liberty of calling the man in question. He confirmed that he'd decided to put off proposing. This news really left a mark on her. It couldn't happen like that. She thought of the sequence of events. The marriage was going to be put off. And maybe a lot of events were going to be changed like that? It upset her to think that all these lives were going to be different. She thought, If I fix them, it's as if it never happened. If I fix them, I'll be able to go back to a normal life.

———

She went into the back of the shop to put together the same bouquet. Then she got into a taxi. "Is it for a wedding?" the driver asked her.

"No."

"For a birthday?"

"No."

"For . . . a graduation?"

"No. It's just for doing what I ought to have done the day I ran somebody over."

The driver continued the journey in silence. Charlotte got out. Put the flowers on the woman's doormat. She stayed there before that image for a moment. Then decided to take a few roses out of the bouquet. She left with them and climbed into another taxi. Since the day of the accident, she'd kept François's address with her. She'd preferred not to meet Natalie, and it was definitely the right decision. It would have been even harder to pull her own life back together if she'd put a face to a shattered life. But at that moment, she was carried away by an impulse. She didn't want to think. The taxi drove along; now it was stopping. For the second time in the past few minutes, Charlotte found herself on a woman's landing. She placed those few white flowers in front of Natalie's door.

Twenty-one

Natalie opened the door and asked herself: was it the right moment? François had been dead for three months. Three months, so few of them. She didn't feel the slightest bit better. On her body, the sentinels of death paraded nonstop. Her friends had advised her to start working again, not to let herself go, to occupy her time to keep it from becoming unbearable. She knew very well that this wouldn't change anything, that it might even make it worse, especially evenings when she got back from work and he wasn't there, wouldn't ever be there. *Not to let yourself go*, what a strange expression. You're letting yourself go whatever happens. Life is about letting yourself go. That was all she wanted: to let herself go; or rather, to let go. To stop feeling the weight of each second. She wanted to rediscover lightness, be it unbearable.

She hadn't wanted to telephone before coming. She wanted to arrive just like that, spontaneously, which would also make the event less of a to-do. In the lobby, elevator, hallways, she'd run into a lot of her coworkers, and all of them had tried as best they could to show her a little warmth as she went by. A

word, gesture, smile, silence sometimes. There were as many at-
titudes as there were people, but she'd been deeply touched by
their unanimous, discreet way of supporting her. Paradoxically,
it was also all these demonstrations that were now making her
hesitate. Did she want that? Did she want to live in an environment where everything was nothing but compassion and uneasiness? If she came back, she'd have to play-act her life, see to
it that everything went all right. She wouldn't be able to stand
seeing kindness in the eyes of others if it led directly to pity.

She was stuck at the door to her boss's office, unable to make
up her mind. She sensed that if she walked in, it would mean
she was definitely returning. Finally, she decided, and walked in
without knocking. Charles was absorbed in reading the dictionary. It was a fetish of his; every morning, he read a definition.

"How are you? I'm not bothering you, am I?" asked Natalie.

He looked up, surprised to see her. She was like a ghost.
Something caught in his throat, he was afraid he couldn't move,
was paralyzed with emotion. She walked up to him.

"You were reading your definition?"

"Yes."

"What is it today?"

"The word *delicacy*. It's not surprising that you appeared at
that moment."

"It's a lovely word."

"I'm glad to see you—here. Well. I was hoping that you'd
come."

Then there was silence. It was strange, but a moment always
came when they didn't know what to say to each other. And in

those cases, Charles always offered tea. It was like gasoline for their words. Then he continued, in a very excited voice, "I was speaking to the shareholders in Sweden. Did you know that I speak a little Swedish now?"

"No."

"Yes . . . they asked me to learn Swedish . . . just my luck. It's really a shitty language."

" . . . "

"But fine, I really owe that to them. They're actually flexible enough . . . anyway . . . yes, I'm telling you this . . . because I spoke to them about you . . . and everybody agreed to do exactly as you choose. If you decide to come back, you'll be able to do it at your own pace, as you wish."

"How nice."

"It's not only nice. We miss you here, really."

" . . . "

"I miss you."

He said it as he stared at her intensely. The kind of insistent look that makes you feel uncomfortable. In an eye, time can go on forever; a second becomes a discourse. To be honest, he couldn't deny two things: he'd always been attracted to her, and his attraction was more pronounced since the death of her husband. It was difficult to admit this kind of affection. Was it a morbid affinity? No, not necessarily. It was her face. It looked as though it had been purified by her tragedy. Natalie's sadness considerably deepened her erotic potential.

Twenty-two

❖ ❖ ❖

Dictionary Definition of Delicacy

1. The quality or condition of being delicate, fragile, or sensitive.
2. Discretion, tact.

Twenty-three

Natalie was sitting at her desk. From the first morning of her return to work, she'd been confronted by something terrible: a block calendar. Out of respect, no one had touched her belongings. And no one had imagined how grim it would be for her to see the date of her last workday before the tragedy frozen in time on her desk. The date two days before her husband's accident. On that page he was still alive. She picked up the calendar and began to turn pages. The days paraded by under her eyes. Each day since François's death had felt loaded with an immense weight. And now, in a few seconds, just by turning the page for each day, she could see the trajectory concretely. All these pages, and she was still here. And now, it was today.

And then, the moment came when there was a new block calendar.

Natalie had been back to work for several months. Some thought the effort she was putting into it was excessive. Time seemed to go back to its course. Everything started again: the routine of meetings, the absurd side of files that you numbered like a series of items without the slightest importance. And then, the height of absurdity: these files would survive us. Yes, this is what she told herself as she filed documents. That all those hunks of pulp were superior to us in many respects, that they weren't subject to illness, old age, or accident. No report would ever get run over while jogging on a Sunday.

Twenty-four

Definition of the Word Delicate,
Since Defining Delicacy *Isn't Enough for*
Understanding Delicacy

1. Subtle and subdued. *A delicate flavor.*
2. Showing fragility. *Delicate crystal.*
3. Requiring sensitive or careful handling. *Delicate situation.*
4. Characterized by subtle judgment, deftness. *Delicate chess maneuvers.*

Twenty-five

❂ ❂ ❂

Since Natalie's return to work, Charles had been in good spirits. He even enjoyed his Swedish lessons from time to time. Something having to do with confidence and respect had been forged between them. Natalie knew the value of the luck she had working for such a benevolent man. But she wasn't duped by it anymore; she sensed his attraction to her. She allowed him to allude to it, as long as he did so more or less subtly. He never went too far, because she'd established a distance that seemed insurmountable to him. She never took part in his game, simply because she couldn't play. It was beyond her power. She was saving all her energy for work. On numerous occasions, he tried to invite her to dinner; each attempt was futile, dismissed by silence. She just couldn't go out. Certainly not with a man. This seemed ridiculous to her; if she had the pluck to hold out all day, concentrating on files that had no importance, why wouldn't she grant herself a few moments of respite? It had to have something to do with her notion of pleasure. She didn't feel she had the right to do anything that was lighthearted. That's how it was. She just couldn't. She wasn't even sure she ever could.

———

Tonight, things were different. She'd finally accepted, and they were going to dinner. Charles had unveiled an unbeatable strategy: they had to celebrate her promotion. Yes, it was true, she'd taken a truly envious step up the ladder and would now manage a team of six people. Although her promotion was completely justified by her competence, she wondered all the same if she'd been given it because of the pity she aroused. At first she'd wanted to say no, but not accepting a promotion was complicated. Then, perceiving Charles's eagerness to arrange that evening, she began wondering whether he'd speeded up her career advancement just to get her to go to dinner. Anything was possible; it was useless to try to understand. She only told herself that he was right: this definitely was a good excuse to force herself to go out. Maybe she'd be able to revive a kind of nightlife nonchalance.

Twenty-six

❀   ❀   ❀

Charles had a major stake in this dinner. He knew it would be decisive. He'd gotten ready for it with the same butterflies in the stomach he'd had for his first date as a teenager. Well, that hadn't been such a crazy feeling. But with Natalie, he could almost imagine he was dining with a woman for the first time. It was as if she possessed the strange knack of wiping out all memories of his love life.

Charles had been careful to avoid candlelit restaurants, to keep from coming on too strongly in the romantic sense, something she might have seen as inappropriate. The first few minutes were perfect. They drank and the conversation was sparse, ending occasionally in brief silences that didn't make them ill at ease. She was glad to be there, having a drink, and thought that she should have gone out earlier, that action led to pleasure. She even wanted to get drunk. Yet something kept her feet on the ground. She could never truly escape her condition. She could drink as much as she wanted, but it wouldn't change anything. She was just there, in a state of complete lucidity, watching herself perform like an actress on a stage. Splitting herself in two, she was dumbfounded to see the woman she no longer was, someone who could exist in life, who could project appeal. It put all the details of her inability to exist in an even harsher light. But Charles saw nothing. He was in his element, taking things literally, trying to make her drink, to gain access to a little life with her. He was enthralled. For months, he'd experienced her as Russian. He didn't really know what that meant, but that's the way it was: in his mind, she had a Russian kind of strength, a Russian sadness. Therefore, her femininity had migrated from Switzerland to Russia.

"So . . . why the promotion?" she asked.

"Because your work is fantastic . . . and I find you wonderful—that's all."

"Really?"

"Why are you asking? You think that's not all?"

"Me? I don't think anything."

"And if I put my hand there, you don't feel anything?"

He didn't know what had given him the nerve. He'd been telling himself that anything was conceivable tonight. How could he be so out of touch? As he placed his hand on hers, he immediately remembered the moment when he'd put it on her knee. She'd looked at him in the same way. And all he could do was withdraw it. He was tired of banging his head against a wall, of living permanently in the unspoken. He wanted to clarify things.

"You're not attracted to me, is that it?"

"But . . . why are you asking me that?"

"What about you? Why these questions? Why don't you ever answer?"

"Because I don't know . . ."

"Don't you think it's time to move forward? I'm not asking you to forget François . . . but you don't want to spend your entire life shut away . . . you know how much I could be there for you . . ."

" . . . But you're married . . ."

Charles was startled to hear her mention his wife in that way. Maybe it seemed crazy, but he'd forgotten her. He wasn't a married man having dinner with another woman. He was a man in the present tense. Yes, he was married. He was living in a state that he referred to as *conjugalease*. His marriage was in stasis. So he was surprised, because he was being profoundly sincere about his attraction to Natalie.

"But why are you talking to me about my wife? She's like a shadow! We just brush by each other."

"You wouldn't think so."

"Because appearances are everything for her. When she comes to the office, it's only to parade around. But if you only knew how pathetic it is, if you only knew . . ."

"Then leave her."

"For you, I'd leave her on the spot."

"Not for me . . . for you."

There was a lapse in the conversation, time to take a few breaths, several sips. Natalie had been shocked by his mention of François, that he'd tried to veer onto slippery ground so quickly and with so little finesse. She ended up saying that she wanted to go home. Charles was very aware that he'd gone too far, that he'd spoiled the evening with his admissions. How could he not have seen that this wasn't the moment? That she wasn't ready. It had to go gently, in stages. And he'd taken off at an insane speed, trying to recapture years of desire in two minutes. All of it had been caused by the way the evening started. It was that beautiful, promising lead-in that had pushed him into the confidence of men who come on too strong.

He pulled himself together; after all, he had the right to say what he was feeling. It wasn't a crime just to open his heart. And yes, it was true that everything was clumsy with her, that her widowed status complicated a lot of things. It occurred to him that he would have had more luck seducing her at some point if François weren't dead. By dying, he'd set their love in stone. He'd flung them into a static eternity. How could you turn on anything at all in a woman in her condition? A woman living in an immutable world. Really, it was enough to make you ask yourself whether he'd killed himself on purpose to make their love last forever. Some people actually think that passion is bound to end tragically.

Twenty-seven

❖ ❖ ❖

They left the restaurant. Their discomfort was getting worse and worse. Charles couldn't find any clever remark or shaft of wit, or even any out-and-out humor that would have allowed him to make up for things a little. To relax the atmosphere slightly. There was nothing to do; they were stuck. For months Charles had been sensitive and considerate, respectful and loyal, and now all his efforts to be decent were being wiped out because he hadn't known how to control his desire. His body had become a dismembered absurdity, each limb with its own heart. He tried to kiss Natalie on the cheek, to make it casual and friendly, but his neck stiffened. This strangled moment lasted a moment more, like a series of slow pretentious seconds.

Then suddenly, Natalie gave him a big smile. She wanted to make him understand that it all wasn't so serious. That it was better to forget the evening, that was all. She said she wanted to walk a little and left on that pleasant note. Charles kept watching her, his eyes glued to her back. He couldn't move, was frozen in defeat. Natalie grew farther away at the center of his field of vision, got smaller and smaller, but he was the one who was shrinking, growing smaller as he stood there.

That is when Natalie stopped.

And turned around.

Once again she walked toward him. The woman who'd been fading away in his field of vision a moment before grew larger the closer she came. What did she want? He mustn't get carried away. Obviously she'd forgotten her keys, a scarf, or one of those many objects women love to forget. But no, that wasn't it. You could tell by her way of walking. You sensed it had nothing to do with anything material. She was coming toward him to speak, to tell him something. She was walking in an ethereal way, like the heroine of an Italian film from 1967. He wanted to step forward, too, to go toward her. In an excess of romanticism, he imagined that it should begin raining. All the silence at the end of the meal had only been confusion. She was coming back not to speak, but to kiss him. It was extraordinary: at the moment when she'd left, he'd had the intuition that he mustn't move, that she was going to return. Because it was obvious there was something instinctive and simple between them, something strong and fragile that had been there from the beginning. It was undeniable; you had to understand her. It wasn't easy for her. Admitting she felt something despite the fact that her husband had just died. It was appalling, even. And yet, how could they resist? Love stories are often amoral.

She was quite close to him now, flushed, heavenly, the alluring embodiment of tragic femininity. She was there, Natalie, his love.

"I apologize for not having answered earlier . . . I was embarrassed . . ."

"Yes, I understand."

"It's so hard to put in words what I'm feeling."

"I know, Natalie."

"But I think I can give you an answer: I'm not attracted to you. And even, I think, I'm not comfortable with your method of trying to seduce me. I'm positive there'll never be anything between us. Maybe I'm simply incapable anymore of loving someone, but if I ever consider it someday, I know it won't be you."

" . . . "

"I couldn't go home like that. I'd rather it be said."

"It has been said. You said it. Yes, it's been said. If I understand, then you've said it. You did say it, yes."

Natalie watched Charles as he spluttered on. Words left hanging, snapped up one by one by silence. Words like the eyes of a dying man. She made a vague gesture of fondness: a hand on the shoulder. And returned the way she'd come. Left again toward the smaller and smaller Natalie. Charles wanted to stay standing there, and it wasn't easy. He couldn't get over it. Especially the tone she'd used. Completely unaffected, without the slightest nastiness. He had to face facts: she wasn't attracted to him and never would be. He wasn't feeling any anger. It was like the sudden end of something that had made him feel alive for years. The end of a possibility. The evening had followed the voyage of the *Titanic*. Festive at first, then shipwrecked. Truth often had the look of an iceberg. Natalie was still in his field of vision, and he wanted to see her leave as quickly as possible. Even the tiny speck she'd become was inordinately unbearable.

Twenty-eight

❖ ❖ ❖

Charles walked a little, until the parking lot. Once he was in his car, he smoked a cigarette. What he was feeling was a perfect match for the jarringly yellow neon. He pulled out of the parking space and turned on the radio. The announcer was talking about a strange series of ties tonight in League 1 soccer. Everything was coherent. He was like the least interesting of all the sports associations, lost in the most unexciting part of the championship games. He was married, he had a daughter, was in charge of an excellent company, but he felt an immense emptiness. Only the dream of Natalie had the ability to make him feel alive. All of it was over now, obliterated, destroyed, ruined. He could string together a list of synonyms, but it wouldn't change anything now. Then he thought that there was something worse than being rejected by a woman you love: having to come across her every day. Ending up near her in a hallway at any moment. He was thinking of the hallway for a reason. She was beautiful in the offices, but he'd always thought that her eroticism displayed itself more powerfully in the hallways. Yes, in his mind, she was a woman of the hallways. And now he'd just realized that at the end of the hallway he was going to have to make a U-turn.

———

On the other hand, to get home, you must never make a U-turn. Charles's car drove along the street he took every day. You would have thought it was the subway, to the extent that the route radiated sameness. He parked and smoked another cigarette in the lot of his building. As he opened the door to his place, he caught sight of his wife in front of the television. No one would have guessed that Laurence had once possessed a kind of furious sexual energy. Slowly but inevitably she was slipping into the prototype of the depressed bourgeoise. Strangely, Charles was affected by that image. He walked slowly up to the television and turned it off. His wife protested, without very much conviction. He walked over to her and firmly took her arm. She wanted to react, but no sound came from her mouth. Deep down she'd dreamed of this moment, dreamed that her husband would touch her, that he'd stop walking past her as if she no longer existed. Their life together was a daily lesson in self-effacement. Without exchanging a word, they headed toward their bedroom. The bed was made, and suddenly it was unmade. Charles turned Laurence around and lowered her panties. Natalie's rejection had given him the desire to have sex with his wife, even a little violently.

Twenty-nine

❖ ❖ ❖

League 1 Soccer Scores the Evening Charles Understood Natalie Would Never Be Attracted to Him

Auxerre–Marseille: 2-2

*

Lens–Lille: 1-1

*

Toulouse–Sochaux: 1-0

*

Paris SG–Nantes: 1-1

*

Grenoble–Le Mans: 3-3

*

Saint-Étienne–Lyon: 0-0

*

Monaco–Nice: 0-0

*

Rennes–Bordeaux: 0-1

*

Nancy–Caen: 1-1

*

Lorient–Le Havre: 2-2

Thirty

✧　✧　✧

After that dinner, their relationship was no longer the same.
Charles kept his distance, and Natalie understood perfectly.
Rare as their exchanges were, they became strictly professional.
Dealing with their respective files didn't cause much of a problem. Since her promotion, Natalie had been managing a team
of six people.* She'd changed her office, and that had been the
best thing for her. Why hadn't she thought of it before? Was
changing décor enough to change your state of mind? Maybe
she ought to think about moving? But she'd barely imagined the
possibility before she understood that she wouldn't feel up to it.
Mourning possesses a double-edged power, an uncompromising power that propels everything as much toward the necessity
for change as toward the morbid temptation to stay faithful to
the past. So she assigned her professional life the task of looking
to the future. Her new office, on the top floor of the building,
seemed to touch the sky, and she congratulated herself for not
being afraid of heights. Here was one kind of rejoicing that was
simple to do.

---

* Since she'd assumed her new duties, she'd bought three pairs of shoes.

The months that followed were still marked by binge working.
She'd even had two minds about studying Swedish in case she
needed to take on new duties. You couldn't say she was ambi-
tious. She was just trying to use files as a palliative. Her friends
and family were still worried, taking her habit of working too
much as a sign of depression. That theory irritated her to the
max. For her, things were simple: she just wanted to work a lot
to keep from thinking, to live in a void. We struggle the best
we can, and she would have liked those close to her to support
her fight instead of holding forth with their murky theories. She
was proud of what she'd managed to do. She went to the office
even on weekends, brought work home with her, forgot about
hours. Inevitably there'd be a moment when she'd collapse from
exhaustion, but for the time being she was making progress
thanks only to Swedish adrenaline.

Her energy impressed everybody. Since she showed not the
slightest flaw, her coworkers started to forget what she'd been
through. François became a memory for the others, and perhaps this is what he could become for her as well. Her long
hours made her constantly available, especially for the members of her team. Chloé, the last to arrive, was also the youngest.
She in particular loved confiding in Natalie, specifically when
it came to her problems with her boyfriend and her constant
worrying: she was terribly jealous. She knew it was ridiculous, but she couldn't control it and act more rationally. As a
result, something unusual happened: Chloé's stories, tinged as
they were with immaturity, allowed Natalie to reconnect with

a world she'd lost, that of her youth and the fears she'd had about not finding a man she'd enjoy being with. Something in Chloé's words created the impression of a memory taking shape again.

Thirty-one

Excerpt from the Scenario Delicacy

SCENE 31: INTERIOR. BAR.

Natalie and Chloé* walk into a bar. It isn't the first time they've come to this place. Natalie follows behind Chloé. They sit down in a corner near a window.

Exterior: the possibility of rain.

CHLOÉ *(in a very spontaneous way)*: How are you? You okay?
NATALIE: Yes, great.

Chloé studies Natalie.

NATALIE: Why are you looking at me like that?
CHLOÉ: I'd like our relationship to be more equal. For

---

* Actresses imagined by the director: Audrey Tautou as Natalie and Mélanie Bernier as Chloé.

you to talk to me about you. It's true that we only talk
about me.

NATALIE: What do you want to know?

CHLOÉ: Your husband has been dead for a long time . . . and
. . . and . . . does it bother you to talk about it?

Natalie seems surprised. Nobody brings up the subject that directly.
There's a pause, and Chloé continues.

CHLOÉ: It's true . . . you're young, beautiful . . . and look at
that man over there—he hasn't stopped looking at you
since we came into the bar.

Natalie turns her head, and her eyes meet those of the man who is
looking at her.

CHLOÉ: He's really not bad, I think. I bet he's a Scorpio. And
since you're a Pisces, it's perfect.

NATALIE: I've barely seen him, and you're already making
predictions?

CHLOÉ: Well, astrology's important. It's the key to my problem with my boyfriend.

NATALIE: Then nothing can be done? He can't change his
sign.

CHLOÉ: No, that idiot will always be a Taurus.

Shot of Natalie's expressionless face.

CUT

Thirty-two

❖ ❖ ❖

Natalie felt ridiculous being here and having this kind of discussion with so young a woman. Moreover, as usual, she wasn't able to live in the moment. Maybe that's what grief is: a permanent disconnect from the here and now. She looked at the games adults played and felt detached. It was easy to tell herself: "I'm not here." Chloé was speaking to her with the rash energy of the here and now, trying to keep her there and push her into thinking, "I am here." She kept talking about that man. And quite rightly, since he was finishing his beer and looking like he was trying to decide whether to approach them. But passing from a glance to a conversation, from the eye to the word, is never simple. After a long day of work, he was in that leisurely mood that sometimes pushes you into bold behavior. Under every daring move, fatigue often hides. He was still looking at Natalie. What did he really have to lose? Nothing, except perhaps a little of the appeal he had from being unknown.

He paid for his drink and left his observation post. His walk could almost have been called resolute. Natalie was several feet away from him: ten, twelve, not more. It dawned on her that this man was coming over to see her. Immediately a strange thought popped into her head: in seven years this man coming toward me may die by being run over. That flash of an idea shook her up inescapably and emphasized her fragility. Every man who approached her ineluctably reminded her of meeting François. However, this one had nothing in common with her husband. He was coming at her with his bedroom smile, his smile from an easy world. But once he got to the table, he was mute. A moment left hanging. He'd made up his mind to come up to them but hadn't prepared the slightest conversation starter. Maybe he was just worried? Surprised, the girls took stock of the man, who stuck there like an exclamation point.

"Hello . . . can I offer you a drink?" he finally let out uninspiredly.

Chloé accepted, and he sat down near them with his feeling of being halfway to the prize. Once he'd sat down, Natalie thought, He's stupid. He offers me a drink when mine has hardly been touched. Then, suddenly, she changed her mind. She told herself that his hesitation at the moment of approaching them was touching. Then once more aggression took the fore. Incessantly shifting, contradictory moods gripped her. She simply did not know what to think. Each of her gestures was quashed by an impulse against it.

Chloé took charge of the conversation, piling on positive stories about Natalie, building her up. To hear her, this was a modern, brilliant, amusing, cultivated, dynamic, scrupulous, generous, uncompromising woman. All of it in under five minutes, so complete that the man only had one question in mind: what was the hitch? During each of Chloé's lyric transports, Natalie had tried to emit believable smiles, to relax the planes of her face, and in rare flashes, she seemed natural. But the energy had drained her. Why put on a face? Why use all her strength to seem affable and agreeable? And then, what would come next? Another date? The need to be more and more candid? Suddenly, everything that was simple and easy was cast in a dark light. Underneath a harmless conversation, she could detect the monstrous mechanism of the life of the couple.

She excused herself and got up to go to the ladies' room. For a long moment, she examined herself in the mirror. Every detail of her face. She splashed a little water on her cheeks. Did she think she was beautiful? Did she have an opinion about herself? About her femininity? It was time to go back. But she stayed there for several minutes without moving, thinking, afloat in her reflections. When she got back to her table, she grabbed her coat. She made an excuse, without taking the trouble to make it seem believable. Chloé said something that she didn't hear. She was already outside. A little later, as he was going to bed, the man wondered if he'd made a fool of himself.

Thirty-three

❖ ❖ ❖

Astrological Signs of the People on Natalie's Team

Chloé: Libra

✳

Jean-Pierre: Pisces

✳

Albert: Taurus

✳

Markus: Scorpio

✳

Marie: Virgo

✳

Benoît: Capricorn

Thirty-four

❖ ❖ ❖

The next morning, she apologized to Chloé without going into detail. At the office, she was Chloé's boss. She was a strong woman. She simply explained that, for the time being, she didn't feel able to go out. "It's too bad," murmured her young colleague. That was all. They had to pass on to something else. After that exchange, Natalie stayed in the hallway for a moment. Then she went back to her office. All the files finally appeared to her under their real light: holding absolutely no interest.

She had never completely withdrawn from the world of the senses. She had never really stopped being a woman, even during moments when she wanted to die. Maybe it was homage to François, or merely came from the idea that sometimes it's enough to put on makeup to seem alive. He'd been dead for three years. Three years of frittering away a life lived in emptiness. They'd often suggested that she leave her memories behind. Maybe it was the best way to stop living in the past. She remembered the expression: *leaving your memories behind*. How do you give up a memory? She'd accepted the idea when it came to objects. She couldn't tolerate having those he'd touched around her anymore. As a result, there wasn't much left, except for a photo she'd put away in the big drawer of her desk. A photo that seemed lost. She looked at it often, as if she were persuading herself that their story had really existed. In the drawer, there was also a small mirror. She took it out to take a look at herself the way a man would if he were seeing her for the very first time. She got up, began walking back and forth in her office, her hands on her hips. Because of the carpeting, her spike heels made no noise. Carpeting can murder sensuality. Who could have possibly invented the wall-to-wall carpet?

Thirty-five

❖ ❖ ❖

Someone knocked. Discreetly, with two knuckles, not more. Natalie gave a start as if those last few seconds had made her believe she could be alone in the world. She said, "Come in," and Markus entered. He was a fellow employee from Uppsala, a Swedish city that doesn't interest many people. Even the inhabitants of Uppsala* themselves are embarrassed; the name of their city sounds almost like an excuse. Sweden has the highest suicide rate in the world. One alternative to suicide is emigrating to France, something Markus must have thought of. Physically, he was rather unpleasant, which is not to say that he was ugly. His way of dressing was always a bit odd: you couldn't tell if he'd salvaged his clothes from his grandfather, at an Emmaus shop, or at a hip secondhand store. All of it formed an ensemble that wasn't very coordinated.

"I came to see you about file 114," he said.

His appearance was weird enough; did he also have to come out with statements as foolish as that? Natalie had no desire to

---

* Of course, it's possible to be born in Uppsala and become Ingmar Bergman. That said, his films should give some idea of the tenor of that city.

work today. It was the first time in a long stretch. She was feeling something resembling despair; would have almost been ready to go on vacation in Uppsala, in other words. She was staring at Markus, who wasn't moving. He was looking at her in amazement. For him, she represented a certain kind of inaccessible woman, doubled by the fantasy that some people develop toward all superiors, or anyone in a position to hold sway over them. So she decided to walk toward him, slowly, very slowly. You'd almost have had the time to read a novel while she made her approach. She seemed not to want to stop, so much so that she found herself nose to nose with Markus, so close that their noses really did touch. The Swede had stopped breathing. What did she want? He didn't have the time to formulate that question in his mind at greater length, because she'd begun to kiss him for all she was worth. It was a long, intense kiss, the intensely adolescent kind. Then suddenly she pulled away.

"We'll see about file 114 later."

She opened the door and suggested Markus leave. Which he did with difficulty. He was Armstrong on the moon. That kiss was one giant leap for mankind—for him. He stayed there at the door to her office for a moment, without moving. Natalie herself had already completely forgotten what had just happened. What she'd just done had no connection to the series of other actions in her life. This kiss was the expression of a sudden insurrection among her neurons, what could be called a gratuitous act.

Thirty-six

❀ ❀ ❀

The Invention of the Wall-to-Wall Carpet

It appears difficult to discover who invented the wall-to-wall carpet. According to the Larousse dictionary, the carpet is merely "a rug sold by the yard."

Here we have an expression that offers undeniable proof of the pathetic nature of the wall-to-wall carpet, which has no relationship to *calling somebody on the carpet.*

Thirty-seven

❖ ❖ ❖

Markus was a punctual man and loved to get home at exactly seven fifteen. He knew the schedules of the suburban trains like other people know their wife's favorite perfumes. He wasn't un-happy with his well-oiled daily schedule. Sometimes he would get the impression that he was friends with the unknown people he ran into each day. That evening, he wanted to shout and tell everybody about his life. His life with Natalie's lips on his lips. He wanted to get up and get off at the first station that came, just like that, to give himself the feeling of deviating from the usual. He wanted to be crazy, which was excellent proof that he was not.

As he walked home, images of his Swedish childhood came back to him. It certainly had happened fast. Childhood in Sweden is like old age in Switzerland. All the same, he remembered those moments when he'd sit at the very rear of the class, just to look at girls' backs. During those years, he'd admired the napes of Kristina's, Pernilla's, and Joana's necks, and those of so many other girls in row A, without ever being able to come anywhere near all the other letters. He didn't remember their faces. He dreamed of finding them, just to tell them that Natalie had kissed him. To tell them that they hadn't been able to see his charm. Ah, how sweet.

When he reached his building, he hesitated. We're forced to memorize so many numbers. Cell phones, Internet access codes, bank cards . . . so, inevitably, there comes a moment when everything gets mixed up. You try to get into your building by punching in your telephone number. Markus, whose brain was perfectly organized, felt as if he were at the threshold of this kind of derailment, and that's exactly what happened to him that night. It was impossible to remember the door code. In vain he tried several combinations. How can you forget by evening something you knew perfectly that morning? Will the welter of data unavoidably push us into amnesia? Finally, a neighbor arrived and stood in front of the door. He could have opened it immediately but preferred to savor this moment of obvious one-upmanship. From the look in his eyes, you'd almost have thought that *remembering your door code* was a sign of virility. Finally the neighbor got moving, pompously declaring, "Please, after you." Markus thought, You stupid ass, if you only knew what was going on in my head; I've got something so beautiful it obliterates useless data . . . He took the stairs, immediately forgetting about this hapless setback. He still felt just as light-headed, and a loop of the scene of the kiss kept playing in his head. It was already a cult film in his memory. Finally he opened the door to his apartment and found his living room much too small in comparison with his appetite for living.

Thirty-eight

❖ ❖ ❖

Code for the Door to Markus's Building

A9624

Thirty-nine

❀ ❀ ❀

The next morning, he got up early. So early that he wasn't even certain he'd slept. He waited impatiently for the sun, as if it were an important date. What was going to happen today? What kind of mood would Natalie be in? And what should he do? Who knew what to do when a beautiful woman kisses you without giving the slightest reason for it? Questions bombarded his mind, and that was never a good sign. He needed to take some calm in-and-out breaths (. . .) and (. . .), whew, like that (. . .), very good (. . .). And tell himself that it was just a day like any other.

Markus loved to read. It was a nice point in common with Natalie. He used his trips on the suburban railway to satisfy that passion. He'd recently bought a number of books and had to choose the one that was going with him on this great day. There was that Russian author he liked a lot, an author who was read markedly less than Tolstoy or Dostoevsky, for no real reason, but it was too bulky a book. He wanted a text he could peck away at when he felt like it, because he knew he wouldn't be able to concentrate. That's why he chose Cioran's *Syllogisms of Bitterness.*

———

Once he arrived, he tried to spend as much time as possible near the coffee machine. To make it seem normal, he drank several cups. After an hour of this, he began to feel a little too worked up. Black coffee and white nights with no sleep were never a good combination. He went to the men's room, felt peaked. Went back to his office. No meeting with Natalie was planned for today. Maybe he should just go and see her? Use file 114 as an excuse. But there was nothing to say about file 114. It would be stupid. He was fed up with letting himself be eaten away by indecision. After all, she was the one who should come! She was the one who'd kissed him. You had no right to act like that without giving an explanation. It was like stealing something and then running away. It was exactly that: she'd run away from his lips. However, he knew she wouldn't come to see him. Maybe she'd even forgotten that moment; for her was it just a gratuitous act? He had good intuition. He sensed a terrible injustice in that possibility: how could the act of kissing be gratuitous for her while it was inestimable for him? Yes, priceless. That kiss was everywhere in him, storming his body.

Forty

❖ ❖ ❖

Excerpt from an Interpretation of the Painting
The Kiss by Gustav Klimt

Most of Klimt's work gives rise to a host of interpretations, but his earlier use of the theme of the embracing couple in the Beethoven frieze and the Stoclet frieze allows us to see in *The Kiss* the ultimate accomplishment of the human quest for happiness.

Forty-one

❖ ❖ ❖

Markus couldn't concentrate. He wanted his explanation. There was only one way to get it: create a fake coincidence. Keep going back and forth in front of Natalie's office—all day, if he had to. There'd have to be a moment when she came out and . . . bam . . . he'd be there, by pure coincidence, walking in front of her office. By the end of the morning, he was drenched in sweat. Suddenly he thought, This isn't my best day! If she walked out now, she'd come across a man dripping sweat who was frittering away his time walking through the hallway without doing anything. He was going to seem like somebody who walks around aimlessly.

After lunch, his thoughts from the morning returned with a vengeance. His strategy was good, and he had to keep up his back-and-forths. It was the only solution. It's really hard to keep walking and pretend you're going somewhere. You've got to look focused, as though you have a clear aim in mind; the hardest part's faking a brisk manner. At the end of the afternoon, when he was worn out, he ran into Chloé. She asked him, "Are you okay? You're acting really weird . . ."

"Yes, yes, I'm okay. I'm getting back the circulation in my legs. Helps me think."

"Still on 114?"

"Yes."

"And it's going okay?"

"Yes, it's okay. More or less."

"Say, I've got nothing but problems with 108. I wanted to talk to Natalie about it, but she isn't here today."

"Oh, really? She . . . isn't here?" asked Markus.

"No . . . I think she's out of town. All right, gotta go; I'm going to try to take care of it."

Markus stood there without reacting.

He'd walked so much that he could have ended up out of town, too.

Forty-two

❖   ❖   ❖

Three Aphorisms by Cioran
Read by Markus on the Suburban Train

The art of love?
It's knowing how to combine the temperament of a vampire
with the discretion of an anemone.

*

A monk and a butcher are wrangling inside

every desire.

*

Sperm is the purest form of bandit.

Forty-three

❖   ❖   ❖

The next day, Markus arrived at the office in a completely different state of mind. He couldn't understand why he'd acted like such a crackpot. What an idea, going back and forth like that. The kiss certainly was disturbing, and he had to admit that lately his love life had been especially uneventful, but that was no reason for acting so childish. He should have kept his cool. He still wanted an explanation from Natalie, but he would no longer try to run into her by faking a coincidence. He'd merely go and see her.

He rapped on the door to her office with a firm hand. "Come in," she said, and he walked in unflinchingly. But then he had to face a major problem: she'd gone to the hairdresser's. Markus had always been very sensitive when it came to hair. And now he was faced with a disconcerting sight: Natalie's hair was wonderfully sleek. Of an astonishing beauty. If only she'd tied it back, as she did sometimes, everything would have been simpler. But in the face of such a capillary revelation, he felt at a loss for words.

"Yes, Markus, what is it?"

Interrupting the rush of thoughts in his mind, he ended up saying the first sentence that popped into his head:

"I really like your hair."

"Thanks, that's nice."

"No, I mean, I adore it."

Natalie was surprised by such an early morning admission. She didn't know whether to smile or get embarrassed.

"Okay, and so?"

" . . . "

"You certainly didn't come to see me just to talk about my hair?"

"No . . . no . . ."

"All right, then. I'm listening."

" . . . "

"Markus, are you there?"

"Yes . . ."

"Well?"

"I'd like to know why you kissed me."

The memory of the kiss returned to the foreground of her memory. How had she been able to forget it? Each instant was being pieced together again, and she couldn't hold in a pout of disgust. Was she crazy? For three years, she hadn't approached a single man, hadn't even thought about being interested in anybody, and then she goes kissing this inconsequential coworker. He was waiting for an answer, which was perfectly understandable. Time was passing. She had to say something.

"I don't know," murmured Natalie.

Markus would have preferred any answer, even a rejection, to this nothing of an answer.

"You don't know?"

"No, I don't."

"You can't leave it like that. You need to explain it to me."

There was nothing to say.

This kiss was like modern art.

Forty-four

❖ ❖ ❖

Title of a Painting by Kazimir Malevich

White on White (1918)

Forty-five

❖ ❖ ❖

Afterward, she thought about it: why that kiss? It just happened.
We're not the masters of our biological clock. In this instance
it was the one that concerns mourning. She'd wanted to die,
had tried to breathe again, had succeeded, then was able to
eat, had even succeeded in going back to work, smiling, being
strong, affable, feminine; and then time had passed with that
wobbly energy of reconstruction, until the day she'd gone into
that bar but fled, unable to bear the cruising game, certain she'd
never be able to be interested in a man; yet the next day, she'd
started walking on the wall-to-wall carpeting, had just done it,
an impulse stolen from doubt; she'd experienced her body as an
object of desire, its shape and hips, and she'd even been disap-
pointed she couldn't hear the sound of her spike heels . . . All of
it had come out of nowhere, the unforeseen birth of a sensation,
a lucid force.

And that was when Markus had entered the room.

There was nothing else to say. Our biological clock isn't rational. It's exactly like an unhappy love affair: you don't know
when you'll get over it. At the most painful moment, you think

that the wound will never heal. And then, one morning, you're startled to discover that you no longer feel this terrible burden. What a surprise to notice that the angst has disappeared. Why on that particular day? Why not later, or sooner? It's the totalitarian decision of our body. Markus shouldn't have looked for a tangible explanation of that impulsive kiss. It had appeared all in good time. Besides, most stories can often be summed up by that simple question of the right moment. Markus, who'd made a mess of so many things in his life, had just discovered his ability to appear in the field of vision of a woman at the perfect moment.

Natalie had read the distress in Markus's eyes. After their last exchange, he'd left slowly. Without making a sound. As unobtrusive as a semicolon in an eight-hundred-page novel. She couldn't leave him like that. She was terribly upset about having acted as she did. She also thought he was a nice man to work with, respectful of everybody, and that made her even more upset about the notion of wounding him. She called him to her office. He put file 114 under his arm, in case she wanted to see him for a work reason. But he didn't give a good goddamn about file 114. In responding to the call, he made a detour by way of the restroom and splashed a little water on his face. Curious about what she was going to say to him, he opened the door to her office.

"Thanks for coming."

"You're welcome."

"I'd like to apologize. I didn't know how to answer. And to be perfectly honest, I still don't know . . ."

" . . . "

"I don't know what came over me. It had to be some kind of physical drive . . . but we work together, and I must say that it was completely inappropriate."

"You sound like an American. That's never a good sign."

She began to laugh. What a strange reply. It was the first time they were talking about anything other than a file. She was discovering a clue to his real personality. She had to get ahold of herself.

"I sound like somebody in charge of a six-person team that you belong to. You walked in just as I was daydreaming, and I didn't grasp the real situation at that moment."

"But that moment was the realest of my life," protested Markus without thinking. It had come right out of his heart.

Things weren't going to be simple, thought Natalie. It was best to put a stop to the conversation. Which she rapidly did. Somewhat curtly. Markus didn't seem to understand. He stood stock-still in her office without moving, vainly looking for the strength to leave. The truth was, when she'd called him in ten minutes before, he'd imagined that she might want to kiss him again. He'd wandered into this dream and had just understood once and for all that nothing more was going to happen between them. He'd been crazy to think it would. She'd only kissed him on the spur of the moment. It was difficult to admit. It was like somebody offering you happiness and then immediately taking it back. He wished he'd never known the taste of Natalie's lips. He wished he'd never experienced that moment, because he was deeply aware that he'd need months to get over those few seconds.

———

Markus headed for the door. Natalie was surprised to catch a tear forming in his eye. It hadn't flowed yet, was waiting to come sliding out in the hallway. He wanted to hold it back. Certainly didn't want to weep in front of Natalie. This was stupid, but the tear he was going to weep was unexpected.

It was the third time he'd wept in front of a woman.

Forty-six

❁ ❁ ❁

Thought of a Polish Philosopher

There are incredible people
whom we meet at the wrong moment.
And there are people who are incredible
because we meet them at the right moment.

Forty-seven

❖ ❖ ❖

Little Love Story About Markus, Told Through His Tears

First and foremost, in this case, let's disregard childhood tears, tears in front of his mother or schoolteacher. This is only about Markus's romantically motivated tears. And so, before that tear he'd tried to control in front of Natalie, there had already been two other occasions.

The first tear went back to his life in Sweden, with a young girl answering to the sweet name of Marilyn. Not a very Swedish name, but surely, Marilyn Monroe respects no boundaries. Marilyn's father had fantasized about this myth his entire life and hadn't found any better idea than naming his daughter after it. Let us say no more about the psychological danger of naming a daughter in honor of one's erotic fantasies. Marilyn's family history is rather immaterial for us, isn't it?

Marilyn belonged to that curious category of women who know their own mind. Regardless of the subject, she could always keep from voicing the slightest uncertain opinion. It was the same when it came to her beauty: every morning, she rose with stardom on her face. Perfectly sure of herself, she always sat in the first row, sometimes trying to undermine male teachers by playfully using her obvious charms to deflect issues of geopolitics. When she entered a room, men fantasized immediately, and women instinctively detested her. She was the subject of every fantasy, which ended up getting on her nerves. Then she came up with a brilliant inspiration for throwing cold water on their enthusiasm: going out with the most insignificant boy. This would unnerve the males, and reassure the girls. Markus was the lucky elect, without understanding why the center of the universe was suddenly taking an interest in him. It was like the United States inviting Liechtenstein to lunch. She showered some compliments on him, claimed she looked at him a lot.

"But how can you see me? I'm always at the back of the class, and you're always in the first row."

"The back of my neck told me everything. There are eyes in the back of my neck," said Marilyn.

Their understanding was born from this exchange.

An understanding that set tongues wagging. That evening, they left high school together under the flabbergasted eyes of everybody. During that period in time, Markus's self-awareness was still not very acute. He knew he had a rather unattractive body, but being with a pretty woman didn't strike him as uncanny. He'd always heard, "Women aren't as superficial as men; for them looks count less. The important thing is to be cultured and amusing." So he'd studied a lot of things and tried to offer proof of his mind. With some success, it should be said; so that his pockmarked face nearly withdrew behind what you'd call a certain charm.

But this charm was shattered when the issue of sex came up. Marilyn certainly had made a lot of effort, but the day when he tried to touch her wonderful breasts, she couldn't control her hand, and her five fingers landed on Markus's astonished cheek. He turned around to look at himself in a mirror and was stupefied by the appearance of red on his white skin. He would always remember this red and associate the color with rejection. Marilyn tried to excuse herself by claiming the gesture had been impulsive, but Markus understood what wasn't being put into words. Something animal and visceral: he disgusted her. He looked at her and began to weep. Each body has its own way of expressing itself.

This was the first time that he cried in front of a woman.

He obtained the Swedish version of an associate's degree and decided to leave for France. A country where the women weren't Marilyn. He'd been hurt by this first romantic episode and had developed a sense of self-protection. Maybe he would follow some path in life that was an alternative to the world of sexuality. He was afraid of suffering, of not being desired, for valid reasons. He was fragile, but had no idea that fragility could be touching to a woman. After three years of urban-style loneliness, despairing of ever finding love, he decided to take part in a speed-dating session. He'd have a chance to meet seven women and talk to each for seven minutes. An infinitely brief time for someone like him: he thought he would need a minimum of a century to convince a sampling of the opposite sex to follow him on the limited path of his life. But something strange happened: during the first encounter, he had the feeling of something in common. The girl's name was Alice,* and she worked in a pharmacy† where she was sometimes responsible for the beauty shop.‡ To tell the truth, it was a simple enough situation: both of them were so uncomfortable with the proceedings that they were able to relax with each other. As a result, their encounter was ideally uncomplicated. After the speed-dating sequence, they hooked up again to extend their seven minutes. Which became days, and then months.

But their story didn't last out the year. Markus adored Alice but didn't love her. Even more importantly, he wasn't attracted to her enough. What a dreadful predicament: for once he'd met someone good, and he absolutely wasn't in love with her. Are we always condemned to the incomplete? During the weeks their relationship lasted, he made some headway in learning about being a couple. He discovered its strengths and its capacity for feeling loved. Because Alice fell madly in love with him. It bordered on the disturbing for someone who'd only known maternal love (and not even that, really). There was something

---

* It's unusual to be named Alice and to end up using this type of function to meet a man. Usually, Alices meet men easily.

† It's unusual to be named Alice and to work in a pharmacy. Usually, Alices work in bookstores or travel agencies.

‡ At this stage, we might ask: was her name really Alice?

very sweet and quietly moving about Markus, a mixture of a kind of strength that reassured and a weakness that melted your heart. And it was exactly that weakness that made him put off the inevitable—leaving Alice. But that is what he finally did one morning. The young woman's suffering wounded him in a remarkably intense way. Perhaps more than his own suffering. He couldn't resist weeping, but he knew it was the right decision. He preferred being alone to digging a larger pit between their hearts.

This was the second time he cried in front of a woman.

For almost two years nothing happened in his life. He'd begun to miss Alice. Especially during subsequent speed-dating sessions, which were especially disappointing—not to say humiliating—when some girls didn't even make the effort to talk to him. As a result, he decided not to go to any more. Had he perhaps given up all thought of living with someone? He was beginning to see nothing interesting about it at this point. After all, there were millions of single people. He could do without a woman. But he was telling himself this as a rationalization, to keep from thinking about how unhappy his situation made him. He dreamed so much about a female body, and sometimes he wore himself out thinking that he'd always be denied it from now on. That he'd lost his passport to beauty.

And suddenly, Natalie had kissed him. His supervisor and an obvious source of fantasy. Then she'd explained to him that it hadn't existed. So he'd just have to get used to it. It wasn't such a big deal, really. Yet he'd wept. Yes, tears had flowed from his eyes, and that had deeply surprised him. *Unexpected* tears. Was he that fragile? No, that wasn't it. He'd taken a worse clobbering many times before. It was just that he'd been especially moved by this kiss; not just for the obvious reason that Natalie was beautiful, but also because of the madness of her action. No one had ever kissed him like that without making an appointment with his lips. That was the magic that had moved him to tears. And now, to the bitter tears of disappointment.

Forty-eight

❖ ❖ ❖

That Friday evening, as he left, he was really glad to be able to take refuge in the weekend. He was going to use Saturday and Sunday as two thick blankets. He didn't want to do anything, didn't even feel like reading. So he put himself in front of the television. That was how he ended up witnessing the speech of the American candidate for president, Barack Obama, on election night in the United States. As Obama himself admitted, he hadn't been the likeliest candidate. Compared to the other frontrunners, he hadn't much money behind him or that many corporate endorsements. It was the people, rather than the political machines, who were going to lead him to victory. And he had galvanized all of them with a simple statement: "Yes, we can." What a fabulous statement, thought Markus. Obama went on to talk about the challenges, setbacks, and false starts he and his supporters would inevitably face. And then he began describing a 106-year-old black woman, born just a generation past slavery, who'd stood in line in Atlanta on election night and cast her ballot. Obama said that, like all of us, she'd seen heartache and hope. And then he repeated the same simple statement, "Yes, we can." After that, he went on to mention all the trials and challenges that his country had faced in the twentieth century, from the First World War to the Great Depression to putting a man on the moon, and he summed it all up once again with the simple sentence, "Yes, we can."

Markus was captivated by the determination of Obama, who was willing to fight with extraordinary—if not to say super-natural—will. In the drive of this political animal he saw every-thing that he was not. And it was indeed on that Saturday night, absorbed in reports about the American presidential election, that he decided to fight. That he decided not to leave things as they were with Natalie. Even if she had told him that all was lost, that nothing could be considered, he continued to believe in it. Whatever it cost, he would be the president and commander in chief of his life.

His first decision was easy: reciprocation. If she'd kissed him without asking, he didn't see why he couldn't do the same. Mon-day morning, first thing, he was going to see her and pay her back in kind with his lips. To do it, he'd stride toward her with a determined step (the most complex part of the strategy: he'd never been very adept when it came to walking with a deter-mined step) and would take hold of her in a virile manner (the other complex part of the strategy: he'd never been very gifted when it came to doing anything at all in a somewhat virile man-ner). In other words, the attack was promising to be compli-cated. But he still had all of Sunday to get ready. A long Sunday of the American Democrats.

Forty-nine

❖ ❖ ❖

President Obama's Remark at the Al Smith Dinner
Regarding the Issue of His National Origin

"Contrary to the rumors you have heard, I was not born in a manger. I was actually born on Krypton and sent here by my father, Jor-El, to save the planet Earth."

Fifty

❖ ❖ ❖

Markus was at Natalie's door. It was time to act, something that plunged him into the most perfect inaction. Benoît, a coworker from his team, walked by.

"Hey, what are you doing?"

"Um . . . I've got a meeting with Natalie."

"And you think you're going to see her by standing stock-still in front of her door?"

"No . . . it's just that we have a ten o'clock meeting . . . and it's nine fifty-nine . . . so, you know me, I don't like to be early . . ."

The coworker walked away feeling more or less the same way he did one day in April 1992. When he'd seen a Samuel Beckett play in a suburban theater.

At that point, Markus was forced to act. He went into Natalie's office. Her head was buried in a file (114, maybe?) and she raised it immediately. He walked toward her with a determined step. But nothing can ever be simple. On the way to Natalie, he had to slow down. His heart was beating harder and harder, in a real Election Day symphony. Natalie wondered what was going to happen. In fact, she was somewhat afraid. However, she was well aware that Markus was niceness incarnate. What did he want? Why wasn't he moving? His body was a computer in need of debugging because of data overload. His data was all emotional. She got up and asked him, "What's happening, Markus?"

" . . . "

"Is everything okay?"

He managed to focus on what he'd come to do. He took her suddenly by the waist and kissed her with energy he didn't know he had. There was no time for her to react before he'd already left the office.

Fifty-one

❊ ❊ ❊

Markus left that strange scene of a stolen kiss behind him. Natalie wanted to plunge back into her report but finally decided to go and look for him. She'd felt something complicated to define. As a matter of fact, this was the first time in three years that someone had taken hold of her like that. Without thinking of her as something fragile. Yes, it was strange, but she'd been shaken up by his hit-and-run, nearly savage gesture of virility. She walked through the hallway asking the employees she passed on her left and her right where he was. No one knew. He hadn't gone back to his office. That was when she thought of the roof of the building. In this season no one went up there, because it was very cold. He had to be there. It was just as she'd thought. There he was near the edge of the roof, looking quite calm. He was making little movements with his lips—puffs, obviously. He looked like he was smoking, but without a cigarette. Natalie walked silently up to him. "I come up here, too, sometimes, to hide. To breathe," she said.

Markus was surprised to see her. He never would have thought she'd go and look for him after what had just happened.

"You're going to catch cold," he replied. "And I don't even have a coat to offer you."

"Well, then, we'll both catch cold. That's at least one way of being that's the same for both of us."

"Clever."

"No, it's not. And the way I acted wasn't clever, either . . . I mean, really, it's not like I committed a crime or something!"

"Then you don't know anything about desire. A kiss from you, and then nothing more, of course it's a crime. Even in the land of hard hearts you'd be convicted."

"The land of hard hearts? . . . That isn't how you usually talk to me."

"I'm certainly not going to break into poetry about 114."

The cold was changing their faces. And aggravating a certain injustice. Markus was becoming slightly blue, not to say pallid, and Natalie was becoming as pale as a depressed princess.

"Maybe it would be better to leave," she said.

"Okay . . . then what'll we do?"

"Well . . . that's enough for now. There's nothing to do. I apologized. We're not going to make a big production out of it, are we?"

"Why not? I wouldn't be opposed to the idea of seeing an extravaganza like that."

"Then we stop. I don't even know what I'm doing talking to you here."

"Okay, we stop. But after we go out to dinner."

"What?"

"We have dinner together. And after that, I promise you we won't talk about it anymore."

"I can't."

"You really owe me that . . . just dinner."

Certain people have the rare ability to come out with such a statement. An ability that keeps the other person from answering in the negative. Natalie sensed all the conviction in Markus's voice. She knew it would be a mistake to accept. She knew she should back away now, before it was too late. But, in front of him, it was impossible to say no. And then, she was so cold.

Fifty-two

❖ ❖ ❖

Concrete Information About
File 114

It consisted of a comparative analysis between France and Sweden of the regulation of the balances of external trade in rural
areas during a period ranging from November 1967 to October
1974.

Fifty-three

❖ ❖ ❖

Markus had gone home first and was pacing in front of his closet. What do you wear to have dinner with Natalie? He wanted to be dressed to the nines. But even that number was too small for her. He would have like to have been dressed to the 47s, or the 112s, or even the 387s. He wanted to deaden himself with numbers to keep from thinking about the pressing issues. Should he wear a tie? He didn't have anyone to help him. He was alone in the world, and the world was Natalie. Usually quite confident about his wardrobe preferences, he was losing his footing in everything and didn't know how to choose the shoes, either. He really had no habit of getting dressed to go out at night. And then, this one was tricky: she was also his supervisor, which added to the pressure. Finally he managed to calm down by telling himself that appearance didn't have to be the most important thing. Above all, he had to seem relaxed and be good at chatting glibly about lots of different subjects. And especially avoid talking about work. The number one taboo would be bringing up file 114. Letting the afternoon rub off on their evening. Then what were they going to talk about? You can't change context with a snap of the fingers. They'd be like two butchers at a vegetarians' convention. No, it was silly. Maybe the best idea was to cancel. There was still time. Unforeseeable circumstances. Yes, sorry, Natalie. You know, I'd really love to have gone, but, well, Mom died today. Nope, that was no good, too brutal. Too Camus, as well; and Camus was no good for canceling. Sartre: a lot better. I can't tonight, you see, because hell is other people. A hint of existentialism in the tone—that would go over nicely. As he raved on, it occurred to him that she must be looking for last-minute excuses, too. But for the moment, still nothing. They were meeting in an hour, and no message. She had to be looking for one, had to be. Or else, maybe there was a problem with her phone battery that was keeping her from notifying him that something had cropped up. His thoughts kept spinning like this a while longer, and then, since there was no news, he went out feeling like he was being asked to perform a mission in space.

Fifty-four

❖ ❖ ❖

He'd chosen an Italian restaurant not far from her place. It was already so nice of her to have dinner with him that he didn't want to make her go across town. Since he was early, he threw down two vodkas at the bistro opposite. He was hoping they would give him a little nerve and get him a little high, too. The alcohol produced no effect, and he went to sit down in the restaurant. Therefore he was in a state of perfect lucidity when he saw Natalie, who was on time. It occurred to him right away that he was glad he wasn't potted. He wouldn't have wanted drunkenness to ruin any of his pleasure in seeing that she'd come. As she walked toward him . . . she was so beautiful . . . the kind of beauty that puts three ellipsis dots after phrases all over the place . . . And then, he thought about the fact that he'd never before seen her in the evening. He was just short of being astounded that she could exist at this hour. He must have been the type who thought that beauty gets put in a box at night. But it couldn't be true, no, because there she was, facing him.

He got up to greet her. She'd never noticed he was that tall. N.B.: Employees sank into the wall-to-wall carpeting at their company. Outside, everybody looked taller. She'd remember this first impression of height for a long time.

"Thanks for coming," Markus couldn't stop himself from saying.

"You're welcome . . ."

"No . . . I mean it, I know you work a lot . . . especially right now . . . with file 114 . . ."

She gave him a look.

He let out an embarrassed laugh.

"Actually, I'd promised myself not to talk about file . . . my God, I'm ridiculous . . ."

Natalie smiled in response. It was the first time since François's death that she'd found herself in the position of having to reassure somebody. It felt good. There was something touching about his embarrassment. She remembered the dinner with Charles, the confidence he'd displayed, and she felt more at ease this time. Having dinner with a man who was looking at her like a politician who's finding out he's won an election he hasn't run in.

"It's better not to talk about work," she said.

"Then what will we talk about? Our interests? Interests are great for starting a discussion."

"Yes . . . but it's a little weird to think like that—about what you can say to each other."

"I think looking for a subject of conversation seems like a good subject of conversation."

She liked that turn of phrase and the way he'd said it. "You're pretty funny."

"Thanks. Do I look as grim as all that?"

"Kind of . . . yeah," she said, smiling.

"Let's get back to interests. That would be better."

"I'm going to tell you something. I don't really think about what I like or don't like anymore."

"Can I ask you a question?"

"Yes."

"Are you nostalgic?"

"I don't think so."

"That's kind of rare for a Natalie."

"Oh, really?"

"Yes, Natalies have a marked tendency for nostalgia."

She smiled again. She wasn't used to it anymore. But this man's words were baffling her a lot. You never knew what he was going to say. The words in his brain seemed like lotto balls before they came out of the machine. Did he have any other theories about her? Nostalgia. She looked frankly at her relationship to nostalgia. All of a sudden Markus had flung her into images from the past. Instinctively she thought of the summer when she was eight. When she'd gone to America with her parents for two fabulous months, traveling all around the West. That vacation was marked by an obsession: Pez. Those little candies that you stack inside figurines. You just push the head and the toy serves you a candy. The identity of one summer was embodied by that object. She never found any again. The memory surfaced in Natalie just as the waiter appeared.

"Would you like to order?" he asked.

"Yes. We'll have two risottos with asparagus. And for dessert . . . we'll have Pez," said Markus.

"You'll have what?"

"Pez."

"We don't have any . . . Pez, sir."

"What a pity," concluded Markus.

The waiter walked away mildly ruffled. In his body, a professional bent and a humorous bent were lines that curved in opposite directions. He couldn't understand what that woman was doing with that man. Beyond a doubt, he was a producer and she an actress. There had to be a professional reason she was having dinner with such a freak. And what was this business about wanting a "pest" for dessert? He hadn't at all liked that reference to bugs. He knew the type of customer who spent his time putting down waiters. That wasn't going to happen.

Natalie was thinking that the evening had taken a delightful turn. Markus was fun to be with.

"You know something? This is only the second time in three years that I've gone out."

"You want to add pressure to pressure?"

"Why, no, everything's fine."

"Glad to hear it. I'm going to see to it that you enjoy the evening, because you'll go back to hibernating if I don't."

Their rapport had very little pretension. Natalie felt good. Markus wasn't a friend or somebody she could see as a future flirtation. He was a realm of comfort, one unconnected to her past. All the conditions for a painless evening had ended up coming together.

Fifty-five

❖ ❖ ❖

Ingredients for Risotto with Asparagus
7 oz. Arborio rice (Italian short-grained rice)

1 lb. 2 oz. asparagus

4 oz. pine nuts

1 onion

7 oz. dry white wine

3 oz. light cream

3 oz. grated Parmesan

hazelnut oil

salt

pepper

*

For the Parmesan Tuiles
3 oz. grated Parmesan

2 oz. pine nuts

2 tablespoons flour

a few drops of water

Fifty-six

❖ ❖ ❖

Markus had often had his eye on Natalie. He loved to see her walking on the wall-to-wall carpeting through the hallways in her spectacular suits. Now her fantasy image was colliding with her real image. Like everyone, he was aware of what she'd been through. However, his only glimpse of her had been what she revealed: a reassuring woman who had a lot of self-assurance. Suddenly discovering her in a context where she had less reason to keep up appearances gave him the feeling he was in touch with her fragility. It's true the change was minimal, but in flashes she lowered her guard. The more she relaxed, the more her real nature showed through. Her weaknesses, having to do with her suffering, came paradoxically to the fore with her smiles. Like the other side of a balance, Markus started taking on a stronger role that came close to being that of the protector. In her presence, he felt amusing and full of life, virile even. He would have liked to lead his entire life with the energy of those moments.

Despite his man-with-the-situation-in-hand suit, his performance had flaws. When he ordered a second bottle, he confused the names of the wines. He'd put on a show of knowing about them, and the waiter hadn't passed up the chance to put in a dig about his ignorance. A little private payback. Markus was more than annoyed enough to dare say to the waiter when he came back with the bottle, "Ah, thank you, sir. We were thirsty. Here's to your health."

"Thank you. That's nice of you."

"No, it isn't. There's a Swedish expression saying that anybody can change places at any time. And that nothing's ever final. So you may be standing up, but will be able to sit down someday. In fact, if you want me to, I'll get up now and give you my place."

Markus stood up abruptly, and the waiter didn't know how to react. He gave a pained smile and left the bottle. Natalie started laughing, without really understanding Markus's mindset. She'd liked that sudden switch into the ludicrous. Giving your seat to the waiter could very well be the best way to put him in his place. She appreciated what she thought of as a poetic moment. She thought Markus had a touch of "the East" in him and found it absolutely charming. It was like Romania or Poland in Sweden.

"Are you sure you're Swedish?" she asked.

"You can't imagine how much I like that question. You're the first person to put my ethnic background in doubt . . . you are truly fabulous."

"Is being Swedish as hard as all that?"

"You can't imagine. When I go back there, everybody tells me I'm a live wire. Do you believe it? Me, a live wire?"

"Certainly."

"Back there, being gloomy is a full-time job."

———

That is how the evening continued, moments of discovery alternating with moments in which a sense of well-being made the other person feel familiar. Although she'd been planning to go home early, it was already past midnight. The people around them were leaving. In a way that was far from subtle, the waiter tried to make them understand that perhaps it was time they think about it, too. Markus got up to go the men's room and paid the bill. The gesture was done with a lot of elegance. Once outside, he offered to take her back in a taxi. He was so considerate. In front of her apartment, he placed a hand on her shoulder and kissed her on the cheek. At that moment he understood what he already knew, that he was desperately in love with her. Natalie thought that every instance of thoughtfulness on his part had shown sensitivity. She had actually felt happy during this time with him. She couldn't think of any other. Lying on her bed, she sent him a text message to thank him. Then she put out the light.

Fifty-seven

❖ ❖ ❖

Natalie's Text Message to Markus
After Their First Dinner

Thanks for the lovely evening.

Fifty-eight

❀ ❀ ❀

His answer was simply, "Thanks for having made it lovely." He had wanted to answer with something that was more original, amusing, moving, romantic, literary, Russian, purple. But in reality, what he did write went very well with the tone of the moment. In his bed, he knew that he wouldn't be able to fall asleep; how could you go into dreamland when you'd just left it?

He managed to sleep a little but was awoken by an anxiety. When a date goes well, you're crazy with joy. And then, little by little, lucidity pushes you to think about what's coming next. If things go badly, at least they're clear: you won't see each other again. But how to deal with this? All the confidence and certainty acquired during dinner had dissolved during the night; you should never close your eyes. A simple occurrence brought this to a head. Early in the day, Natalie and Markus ran into each other in the hallway. One was going to the coffee machine, the other coming back from it. After exchanging self-conscious smiles, they somewhat overplayed greeting each other. Neither of them could say another word, or find an anecdote that could end up in conversation. Not a single thing. Not even a brief mention of the weather, whether it was cloudy, sunny—nothing at all, with no hope of the situation improving. They separated on this feeling of uneasiness. They'd had nothing to say to each other. Some people call this the *sidereal emptiness of afterward*.

In his office, Markus tried to put his mind at rest. It was altogether normal for perfection not to remain constant at all times. Life certainly has its muddled moments, erasures, blank spaces. Put Romeo and Juliet in a hallway the morning after a lovely evening and they definitely won't have a thing to say to each other. No big deal. He should be concentrating on the future instead. That's what's important. And you could say he was coping pretty well. Very quickly, he became absorbed in ideas for evenings, nocturnal strategies. He put it all on a large sheet of paper, like a plan of attack. In his little office, file 114 ceased to exist; file 114 had been obliterated by the file on Natalie. He didn't know whom to talk to about it, whom to ask for advice. He did have good relationships with several coworkers. With Berthier, especially, he shared some personal secrets and vented in a way you could call intimate. But when it was a question of Natalie, talking to anybody at all in this place was out of the question. He'd have to shore up his uncertainties behind a wall of silence. Silence, yes, although he was afraid his heart would beat so loud it would make too much of a racket.

On the Internet, he checked out all the sites with suggestions for romantic evenings, boat excursions (although it was cold) or a night at the theater (though it was often hot inside and, anyway, he couldn't stand plays). He found nothing very exciting that wouldn't seem pompous or not enough so. In other words, he had no idea what she'd want, or what she was thinking. Maybe she didn't want to see him anymore. She'd agreed to go to dinner with him once. Maybe that was it. She'd seen to it that it went okay. Now it was all over. Promises are only valid at the time of the promise. On the other hand, she'd thanked him for the lovely evening. Yes, she had, she'd written the word "lovely." Markus relished that word. That wasn't nothing, "a lovely evening." She could have written "a nice evening," but no, she'd chosen the word "lovely." "Lovely"—what a beautiful word. Clearly, what a lovely evening. It was enough to make you think you were in that heyday of long dresses and horse-drawn carriages . . . But what was I thinking about? he thought, suddenly going into a tailspin. I've got to act and stop letting my mind wander. Yes, "lovely" certainly was beautiful, but it wasn't even a foot in the door; now he needed to shake a leg and go the extra mile. Oh, he felt desperate. He didn't have the slightest idea. Being at ease yesterday was only the ease of one evening. An illusion. He was reverting to his pathetic condition of being a man without qualities, a man without the slightest idea how to set up a second date with Natalie.

There was a knock on the door.

Markus said, "Come in." The person who appeared was the one who'd written about having had a lovely evening with him. Yes, Natalie was there, it was really her.

"You're okay? I'm not interrupting you? You look like you're really absorbed in something."

"Uh . . . no . . . no, it's okay."

"I was wondering if you'd like to go to a play with me tomorrow . . . I've got two tickets . . . so if it's . . ."

"Great. I love the theater."

"Great, then. Tomorrow evening."

He murmured, "Tomorrow night," too, but it was too late. The reply floated in thin air, disturbed by having no ear to land on. Every atom of Markus melted into intense pleasure. And at the center of this ecstatic realm, his heart leapt with joy throughout his entire body.

Strangely, this happiness made him serious. In the subway, he studied every person in his car, all those people stuck in their humdrum days, and no longer really felt anonymous among them. He stood there and, more than ever, knew that he loved women. Once he was home, he went through the steps of his routine. But he didn't feel much like dinner. He lay down on his bed and tried to read a few pages. Then he turned out the light. The only problem was: he couldn't fall asleep, just as he'd barely slept after Natalie's kiss. She'd amputated sleep from his repertoire.

Fifty-nine

❖ ❖ ❖

Excerpt from the Package Insert for Guronsan

For treatment of temporary states of fatigue in adults.

Sixty

❖ ❖ ❖

The day went by easily. There was even a meeting of the team, something normal, and no one had any clue that Natalie was going to see a play that evening with Markus. It was kind of a nice feeling. Employees love having secrets, starting underground affairs, living a life no one knows about. It adds spice to the couple they form with their company. Natalie knew how to compartmentalize things. In certain respects, her tragedy had anesthetized her. Which is to say that she ran the meeting robotically, almost forgetting that the day was leading to an evening out. Markus certainly would have liked seeing some special attention, some sign of intrigue, in Natalie's eyes, but that wasn't part of her m.o.

The same was true of Chloé, who from time to time would have liked others to notice her privileged relationship with their supervisor. She was the only one who spent time with her that could be categorized as "casual." Since Natalie had walked out on her, Chloé hadn't tried to set up a second time out together. She knew the dangerous element that could enter into those moments: witnessing her superior's fragility could backfire. That's why she made a point of not mixing categories and scrupulously respecting hierarchy. At the end of the day, she went to see her.

"How are you? We've hardly talked since the last time."

"Yes, it was my fault, Chloé. But it was a nice time, really."

"Oh, really? You took off like a bat out of hell, and it was a nice time?"

"Yes, I mean it."

"Great, then . . . want to go back there tonight?"

"Oh, no, sorry, I can't. I'm going to a play," said Natalie as if she were announcing the birth of a green baby.

Chloé didn't want to seem surprised, but there certainly was reason to be. It was better not to emphasize the momentous character of such a statement, and to act as if it were nothing. Once back in her office, she lingered a while to put the final elements of her report in order, check her e-mails; then she put on her coat and left. As she was walking to the elevator, she was struck by an improbable sight: Markus and Natalie leaving together. She got nearer to them without being seen. She thought she heard the word "theater." Immediately, she sensed something she couldn't define. Distress, even dislike.

Sixty-one

❖ ❖ ❖

Theater seats are so narrow. Markus definitely wasn't comfortable. He was sorry about having long legs; as regrets go, it certainly was a useless one.* Not to mention another fact that amped up his torture: there's nothing worse than being seated next to a woman you're dying with desire to look at. The show was to his left, where she was, not on stage. Not only that, but what was he seeing? It was so-so. The fact that it was a Swedish play wasn't exactly helping matters! Had she done it on purpose? As if that weren't enough, the playwright had studied in Uppsala. Might as well have dinner at his parents'. He was too distracted to follow whatever the plot was. They were sure to talk about it afterward, and he'd come off as a retard. How could he have forgotten that possibility? He absolutely had to concentrate and prepare a few clever comments.

All the same, at the end of the play, he was surprised to be affected by a strong emotion. Maybe even on the order of a Swedish identification with the work. Natalie seemed content, too.

---

* There are no short legs for rent.

But it's difficult to know at the theater; sometimes people seem happy for the simple reason that the ordeal is finally over. Once they were outside, Markus wanted to launch into the theory he'd constructed during Act III, but Natalie cut the discussion short.

"I think we should try to unwind now."

Markus thought of his legs, but Natalie elucidated, "Let's get a drink."

So that was it, unwind.

Sixty-two

❀ ❀ ❀

Excerpt from **Miss Julie**
by August Strindberg,
the Play Seen by Natalie and Markus
on Their Second Date

JULIE: Shall I obey you?

JEAN: For once—for your own sake. I beg of you. Night is
crawling along, sleepiness makes one irresponsible and the
brain grows hot.*

---

* Translator's note: Translated from the Swedish into English by Edith and
Warner Oland (1912).

Sixty-three

❖ ❖ ❖

Then something decisive happened. An insignificant factor that would enlarge into a major determinant. Everything went exactly as it had during their first evening. Charm took effect, and even progressed. Markus came out of it elegantly. He was smiling with his least Swedish smile possible, almost a kind of Spanish smile. He strung out some tasty anecdotes, skillfully mixed in cultural and personal references, successfully managed transitions from the intimate to the general. He gracefully unfurled a fine piece of engineering known as "man of the world." But, at the heart of his sense of well-being, he was suddenly prisoner of a confusion that was going to derail the machine: he was having an outbreak of melancholy.

At the beginning, it wasn't much at all to deal with, more like a form of nostalgia. But no, as you drew much nearer, you could discern the mauve look of melancholy. And even closer up, you could see the real nature of a certain sadness. From one second to another, like a morbid, pathetic urge, he found himself face to face with the emptiness of that evening. But why am I trying to put on my best face, he asked himself? Why try to make this woman laugh, do my damnedest to delight her, a woman who's so completely inaccessible? His past as a man unsure of himself caught him in its claws. And that wasn't all. The development of this withdrawal was tragically reinforced by a second determinant: he spilled his glass of red wine on the tablecloth. It could have been seen as a simple blunder. Maybe even a charming one; Natalie had always had a spot in her heart for awkwardness. But at the moment, he was no longer thinking of her. He was seeing that trivial event as a much more serious harbinger: the reappearance of red. The never-ending eruption of red in his life.

"It's not such a big deal," said Natalie, noticing Markus's look of catastrophe.

Of course not; it wasn't a big deal. It was tragic. The red sent him back to Marilyn. Back to a vision of all the women in the world who were rejecting him. A snicker droned in his ears. Images of all his apprehensions surfaced again: he was a child being mocked on the school playground, a soldier being hazed, a tourist being swindled. All of it represented by the spreading of the red stain on a white tablecloth. He imagined the world watching him, whispering as he walked by. He was swimming in his too-large suit of a womanizer. Nothing could stop this drift into paranoia. A drift heralded by melancholy, and the simple feeling of seeing the past as a refuge. At that moment, the present stopped existing. Natalie was a shadow, a ghost from the world of women.

Markus rose and was lost in silence for a moment. Natalie watched him, without knowing what he was going to say. Was he going to be funny? Grim? Finally, he declared in a calm tone of voice, "I'd better leave."

"Why? Because of the wine? But . . . that happens to everybody."

"No . . . it's not that . . . it's just . . ."

"Just what? I bore you?"

"But no . . . of course not . . . even dead you couldn't bore me . . ."

"Then what?"

"Then nothing. It's just that I'm attracted to you. I'm attracted to you a lot."

" . . . "

"I have only one desire, to kiss you again . . . but I can't imagine for a single moment your being attracted to me . . . so, I think it would be best for us to stop seeing each other . . . I'm bound to suffer, but that suffering won't be as harsh, if I have the nerve to say . . ."

"You think like that all the time?"

"But how can I not? What do I have to do just to be here, opposite you? Do you know how to do that, do you?"

"Be opposite myself?"

"You see, what I'm saying is idiotic. It would be better for me to leave."

"I'd like you to stay."

"To do what?"

"I don't know."

"What are you trying to do to me?"

"I don't know. I only know that I feel good when I'm with you, that you're unpretentious . . . considerate . . . delicate with me. And I'm realizing that it's what I need, plain and simple."

"And that's all?"

"That's already a lot, isn't it?"

Markus was still standing. Natalie got up, too. They remained like that for a moment, frozen in uncertainty. Heads turned in their direction. It's pretty rare not to move when you're standing. It might bring up the idea of that painting by Magritte with men falling from the sky like stalactites. So there was a bit of Belgian painter in the bearing of the two of them, which isn't, obviously, the most reassuring of images.

Markus left Natalie and walked out of the café. The moment had turned perfect, and he had to escape. She didn't understand his attitude. She'd been having a nice evening, and now, she held this against him. Without realizing it, Markus had acted brilliantly. He'd reawakened Natalie. He'd pushed her into asking herself some questions. He'd said that he wanted to kiss her. Then was that all it was? Did she want to? No, she didn't think so. She didn't find him particularly . . . but that wasn't really important . . . then, why not . . . she thought he had something . . . and he was fun, too . . . then why had he left? What an idiot. Now everything was spoiled. She was deeply annoyed . . . what an idiot he was, yes, what an idiot, she kept repeating while the customers in the café studied her. Such a beautiful woman dumped by a second-rate guy like that. She didn't even notice their glances. She stood there frustrated and annoyed about not having mastered the situation, not having known how to hold him back, how to understand him. There was no reason to blame herself; she wouldn't have been able to do anything. In his eyes, she was much too desirable to be near.

When she got home, she dialed his number, but hung up before it rang. She wanted him to call her. After all, she was the one who'd taken the initiative for this second date. He could have at least thanked her. Sent a message. There she was, waiting in front of the telephone, and it was the first time in so long that she'd experienced such a thing: waiting. She couldn't sleep and poured herself a little wine. Put on some music. Alain Souchon. A song she used to love listening to with François. She couldn't get over being able to listen to it like this without breaking down. She kept walking in circles around the living room, even danced a little, let the feeling of being high enter her with the energy of something promised.

Sixty-four

❖ ❖ ❖

First Verse of "L'amour en fuite" ("Love on the Run"),
the Alain Souchon Song Natalie Listened to After
Her Second Evening with Markus

Loving pictures shot with cameras on my skin,
we lived it.
Tear them up and all those times we cried,
forgive it.
We've got all the glue and sticky tape
To put those broken hearts back into shape.

What images we formed back in those days,
cute couple.
I moved in with you and found your world,
your bubble.
Then came the broken glass that stung our smiles.
Bloody shards of glass on our new tiles.

Me, you, we just couldn't cope.
Boohoo, those tears without hope.
Leavin' each other, and both of us mum.
It's love on the run,
Love on the run.

Sixty-five

❀ ❀ ❀

Markus had walked along the precipice, with the feeling of the wind under his feet. As he went home that evening, he kept being haunted by painful images. Maybe it was all connected to Strindberg? Everyone should avoid coming into contact with the fears of his countrymen. The beauty of the moment, the beauty of Natalie, all of it he'd seen as a final destination: one of devastation. There was beauty before him, looking him straight in the eye, like a foretaste of tragedy. Wasn't that the epigraph in Visconti's film of *Death in Venice*, that crucial sentence: "He who contemplates beauty is destined to death?" Well, yes, Markus could seem bombastic. And even stupid for having run away. But you need to have lived years in nothingness to understand how a person can suddenly become frightened by a possibility.

He hadn't called her. She who had loved his Eastern European side would now get the surprise of discovering once again his adherence to Swedishness. Not the least atom of Polish in him. Markus had decided to shut down and *stop playing with the fires of femininity*. Yes, such were the words cartwheeling through his mind. The first consequence was the following: he decided never to look her in the eye again.

The next morning, as Natalie arrived at the office, she ran into Chloé. Let's admit it on the spot: the latter was also well versed in phony coincidences. Therefore, she just happened to be walking back and forth in the hallway when she encountered her superior.* Blatantly gossipy, with less grace than a porcupine, she was intending to try to pry out a few little secrets.

"Well, hi, Natalie. How're you doing?"

"Fine, I'm okay. Just a little tired."

"Was it the play you saw last night? Was it long?"

"No, not especially . . ."

Chloé sensed that it would be complicated to find out more, but a chance occurrence was going to simplify everything. Markus was approaching, and he as well seemed to be in a strange mood. The young woman made sure he'd stop.

"Oh, hello, Markus, how's it going?"

"Fine, I'm okay . . . how 'bout you?"

"Not bad."

As he answered her he avoided looking at the two women. It made a very strange impression, like talking to somebody in a hurry. Which was weird because, actually, Markus didn't seem hurried at all.

"You okay? Is something the matter with your neck?"

---

* We may finally ask ourselves whether coincidence really does exist. Maybe everybody we run into is walking around near us with the undying hope of meeting us? To think of it, it's a fact that they often seem out of breath.

"No . . . no . . . I'm okay . . . all right, I've got to go."

He walked off, leaving the two women staggered. Immediately Chloé thought, He sure is uncomfortable . . . they have to have slept together . . . I don't see any other explanation . . . if not, why would he have ignored her? So she gave Natalie a big smile.

"Can I ask you a question? Did you go to the theater with Markus yesterday?"

"It has nothing to do with you."

"Fine . . . it's just that I thought we shared things, the two of us. I tell you everything."

"But I don't have anything to say. All right, we'd better get back to work."

Natalie had been terse. She hadn't been pleased by the liberty Chloé had taken. You could easily see an eager quest for gossip in her eyes. Embarrassed, Chloé stammered that she was organizing drinks for tomorrow, which was her birthday. Natalie made a vague gesture that said okay. But she wasn't certain anymore she'd be going.

Later, in her office, she thought again about Chloé's lack of finesse. For months, Natalie had been living with rumors in her wake. Quiet remarks about how well she was holding up, what she was doing, her way of devoting herself to her work. No matter how deeply well-meaning such surveillance was, she'd experienced it as a burden. During that time, she would have preferred not being looked at by anybody. Paradoxically, continual expressions of affection had complicated the task. She had a bitter memory of the time she'd attracted attention. Consequently, as she thought about the way Chloé had spoken, she understood how discreet she would have to be, never mentioning anything about her affair with Markus. But is that what it was, an affair? With the death of François she'd lost all her criteria. She'd felt like an adolescent again. As if everything she knew about love had been ravaged. Her heart beat on these ruins. She didn't understand Markus's attitude, and his way of not looking at her anymore. What an act he was putting on! Either that, or was he nuts? Sheer lunacy was more than probable. She didn't think: you have to really love a woman in order not to want to see her. No, that was something she didn't think. She merely settled into a state of confusion.

Sixty-six

❁　❁　❁

Three Rumors Concerning Björn Andrésen,
the Actor Who Played Tadzio
***in Luchino Visconti's* Death in Venice**

He'd killed a gay actor in New York.

*

He'd died in an airplane crash in Mexico.

*

He would only eat green salad.

Sixty-seven

❖ ❖ ❖

Markus didn't feel like working. He stood at the window, staring into empty space. He was still filled with nostalgia—to be more precise, a ridiculous nostalgia. That illusion that says our gloomy past nevertheless has a certain charm. At that moment, as poor as his childhood had been, it seemed like a source of life to him. He thought about the details of it and found them touching, whereas previously they'd always been lamentable. He was looking for refuge, anywhere at all, as long as it would let him escape the present. However, in the last few days, he'd achieved a sort of romantic dream by going to the theater with a beautiful woman. Then why was he feeling such a strong need to backpedal? Clearly there had to be something easy to understand about it, something you could call *fear of happiness*. They say the most beautiful moments of our life pass before us right before we die. Then it seemed plausible that you could see the havoc and heartbreak of the past parade before you at the moment when happiness comes with its almost unsettling smile.

Natalie had asked him to come by her office, and he'd refused.

"I actually would like to see you," he'd said. "But by telephone."

"See me by telephone? Sure you're okay?"

"I'm okay, thanks. I'm just asking you not to enter my field of vision for several days. That's all I'm asking."

She was getting more and more unnerved. And yet, she could still feel charmed by so much oddness. Her wondering went far afield. She considered the fact that Markus's affectation might be a form of strategy. Or else a modern form of romantic humor. Of course, she was wrong. Markus was completely and distressingly trapped at emotional stage 1.

By the end of the day, she'd decided not to follow his instructions; she went to his office. Immediately, he averted his gaze.

"This won't do! What's more, you're entering without knocking."

"Because I want you to look at me."

"I don't want to."

"Are you always like this? Are you sure it's not because of that glass of red wine?"

"In a way it is."

"You're doing this on purpose? To puzzle me, is that it? I must admit it's working."

"Natalie, I promise you there's nothing else to understand but what I said to you. I'm protecting myself, that's all. That's not difficult to grasp."

"But you're going to get a neck ache staying like that."

"I'd rather have a neck ache than heartache."

She was left hanging with that last phrase, which she heard as some kind of culinary combination, like ham-'n'-eggs, or even an exotic dessert combination like bananas-'n'-cream: *necake-'n'-artake*. Then she went on, "And what if I want to see you? And if I want to spend some time with you? And if I feel good when I'm with you. What do I do?"

"It's not possible. It won't ever be possible. It's better for you to leave."

Natalie didn't know what to do. Should she have kissed him, slapped him, sacked him, ignored him, made a fool of him, begged him? Finally she turned the handle of the door and left.

Sixty-eight

✦ ✦ ✦

At the end of the next day, Chloé celebrated her birthday in the office. She couldn't stand people forgetting it. In a few years, obviously, the opposite would be true. You could appreciate her energy, her way of making a gloomy environment exuberant, her way of pushing the employees who were there into feigned good humor. Practically everyone who worked on the floor was there, and Chloé, who was surrounded by them, was drinking a glass of champagne. Waiting for her gifts. There was something touching, almost charming, in her ridiculously exaggerated display of narcissism.

The room wasn't very big; even so, Markus and Natalie did their best to stay as far away from each other as possible. She'd finally given in to his demand and was trying her best not to appear in his field of vision. Chloé, who was following their little game, wasn't duped. They have a way of not speaking to each other that speaks volumes, is what she thought. Quite perceptive. Well, fine, but she didn't want to become too preoccupied by this affair; making her birthday toast a success, that was obviously the important thing. All the employees, the Benoîts and

Bénédictes, standing there listlessly in suits with glasses in hand and that controlled art of conviviality. Markus studied the small enthusiasms of each and found them grotesque. But for him, the grotesque had a profoundly human aspect. He, too, wanted to be a part of this collective rhythm. He'd felt the need to do things right. Late in the afternoon, he'd ordered white roses by telephone. It was an immense bouquet that was way out of proportion to his relationship with Chloé. Like a need to cling to white. To the immensity of white. A white that made amends for red. Markus had come down when the young woman who was delivering the flowers arrived at reception. An astonishing image: Markus taking hold of a gigantic bouquet in that functional, soulless lobby.

Holding the bouquet, he walked toward Chloé, preceded by a sublime mass of white. She saw him coming and asked, "Is that for me?"

"Yes. Happy birthday, Chloé."

She was embarrassed. Instinctively, she turned her head toward Natalie. Chloé didn't know what to say to Markus. There was a white space between them: their own white on white. Everybody was looking at them. Or rather, what could be seen of their faces, those particles that escaped from the white. Chloé sensed that she had to say something, but what? Finally, "You shouldn't have. It's too much."

"Yes, I know. But I felt like having some white."

Another coworker came up holding a present, and Markus took advantage of this by backing away.

———

Natalie had watched what happened from a distance. She'd wanted to respect Markus's rules, but since she was deeply upset by what she'd seen, she decided to come up to him and speak.

"Why did you give her that kind of bouquet?"

"I don't know."

"Listen . . . I'm starting to get fed up with your autistic put-on . . . you don't want to look at me . . . you don't want to explain things to me."

"I promise you that I don't know. I'm the one who's the most upset. I realize that it's all out of proportion. But that's the way it is. When I ordered flowers, I asked for an immense bouquet of white roses."

"So you're in love with her?"

"Are you jealous or what?"

"I'm not jealous. But I'm beginning to wonder whether there might be a womanizer hiding under your depressive-drops-in-from-Sweden routine."

"And you're . . . an expert in male psyches, no doubt."

"That's completely ridiculous."

"What's ridiculous is that I also have a present for you . . . and that I haven't given it to you."

They studied each other. And Markus said to himself, How could I have thought that I couldn't see her anymore? He smiled at her, and she smiled back. Time again for the waltz of smiles. Amazing how you sometimes make resolutions, tell yourself everything will be a certain way from now on, and then all it takes is a tiny movement of the lips to shatter your confidence in a certainty that seemed eternal. All of Markus's will power had just crumbled when faced with the evidence of Natalie's face. It was a tired face, clouded by incomprehension, but still Natalie's face. Without a word they discreetly left the party and met in Markus's office.

Sixty-nine

❖   ❖   ❖

It was a narrow space. The relief they both felt was enough to fill the room. They were happy to be alone together. Markus studied Natalie, and the hesitation that he read in her eyes went to the depths of him.

"What about this present?" she asked.

"I'll give it to you, but you have to promise me not to open it before you get home."

"All right."

Markus held out a small package, and Natalie put it in her bag. They stayed that way for a moment, the kind of moment that Albert Cohen called *a moment that is still going on.* Markus didn't feel he had to speak, to fill the void. They were relaxed, happy to be together again. After a moment, Natalie said, "Maybe we should go back. It will look strange if we don't."

"You're right."

They left the office and made their way down the hall. Once they got back to where the party was, they had a surprise. No one was there anymore. The party was over, and everything had been put back in place. They began to wonder how much time they'd spent in the office.

Sitting on her couch after she got home, Natalie opened the package. Inside it was a Pez dispenser. She couldn't get over it; you can't find them in France. She was deeply touched by the gesture. She put her coat back on and went out again. With a movement of her arm (a gesture that suddenly seemed simple), she flagged down a taxi.

Seventy

Wikipedia Article About Pez

The name *Pez* was derived from . . . the German word for peppermint, Pfefferminz, the first Pez flavor. Pez was originally introduced in Austria . . . and eventually became available worldwide. The Pez dispenser is one of the characteristics of the brand. Its great variety makes it an object that is highly collectible.

Seventy-one

Once she got to the door, she hesitated for a moment. It was so late. But she'd already come this far; it would be ridiculous to turn around and go back. She rang once, then a second time. Nothing. She began knocking. After a minute, she heard footsteps.

"Who's there?" asked an anxious voice.

"It's me," she answered.

The door opened, and Natalie was disconcerted by what she saw. Her father's hair was disheveled, his eyes haggard. He seemed stunned, a little as if he'd been robbed. Actually, it was probably because he'd had his sleep stolen.

"What are you doing here? Is there a problem?"

"No . . . I'm okay . . . I wanted to see you."

"At this hour?"

"Yes, it was urgent."

Natalie walked into her parents' home.

"Your mother's sleeping, you know. The world could end, and she'd still be sleeping."

"I knew it was you I was waking up."

"You want something to drink? Herbal tea?"

Natalie accepted, and her father went into the kitchen. There was something comforting about the way they related. Now that the surprise was over, her father had recovered his attitude of calm. It felt like he was going to take things in hand. However, at that time of night, Natalie thought to herself that he'd aged. She'd seen it just in his way of walking with slippers. She'd told herself, This is a man who's been awoken in the middle of the night, but he takes the time to put on his slippers to go see what's going on. Such caution about his feet was touching. He came back into the living room.

"So what's happening? What is it that can't wait?"

"I wanted to show you this."

She took the Pez dispenser out of her pocket, and immediately, father experienced the same emotion as daughter. The little object sent them back to the same summer. All of a sudden, his daughter was eight. So she came up to her father and gently put her head on his shoulder. All the affection of the past was in the Pez, everything that had been squandered with the passage of time, too, not suddenly, but here and then there. The Pez held the time before unhappiness, when fragility amounted to a fall, a scratch. The idea of her father was in the Pez, the man she loved to run toward as a child, leaping into his arms; and once she felt him against her, she could think about the future with an extraordinary assurance. The two of them remained in a state of wonder, contemplating the toy, an insignificant, silly little object that was nevertheless so moving, containing as it did all the gradations of life.

———

Then Natalie began to weep. Deeply. The tears of that suffering she'd held back in her father's presence. She didn't know why, but she'd never let go in front of him. Was it because she was an only child? Was it maybe because she'd had to play the role of a boy, too? The one who doesn't weep. But she was a little girl, a child who'd lost her husband. So, after all this time, in the playful aura of the Pez, she began to weep in the arms of her father. To let herself drift into the hope of consolation.

Seventy-two

❖ ❖ ❖

The next day, when Natalie arrived at the office, she was a little sick. She'd ended up sleeping at her parents'. Early in the morning, just before her mother woke up, she'd come back to her own home. Memory of the all-nighters of her youth, those nights when she could party until dawn, change her clothes, and go directly to class. She was experiencing one of the paradoxes of the body: a state of exhaustion that makes you feel awake. She went to see Markus and was surprised to find that he was in exactly the same state of mind as the day before. A sort of calm strength that was exactly the same. The thought of it reassured her, even made her feel relieved.

"I'd like to thank you . . . for the present."

"You're welcome."

"Can I buy you a drink this evening?"

Markus nodded, thinking, I'm in love with her, and she's always the one who takes the initiative for our get-togethers. Above all, he decided he shouldn't be afraid anymore, that he'd been silly to withdraw like that, to protect himself. You should never be stingy about a potential torment. Once again, he kept thinking, even answering her, although she'd already left several minutes ago. He still believed that all of it could lead to suffering, disappointment, the most terrifying emotional impasse that exists. But he wanted to go there. He wanted to leave for an unknown destination. Nothing was tragic. He knew there were ferries between the isle of suffering and that of forgetfulness, and one that was even farther away, hope.

Natalie had suggested they meet at the café. It was better to be discreet after sneaking away the previous day. And she also hadn't forgotten Chloé's questions. This was okay with him, even if, deep down, he could have organized a press conference trumpeting every date with Natalie. He got there first and decided to sit where he could be easily seen. A strategic place designed to prevent anyone from missing the production of the arrival of the beautiful woman with whom he had a date. It was an important act, which certainly shouldn't have been considered superficial. In any case, it had nothing to do with male vanity. Something else that was much more important should have been seen in it: a first achievement of self-acceptance.

That morning, for the first time in a long time, he'd forgotten to take a book with him when he left home. Natalie had told him that she'd come as quickly as possible to the café, but he hadn't ruled out that he'd have to wait for a while. Markus got up to get one of the free papers, and he dove into a reading of it. Soon he was fascinated by a story. He was deeply absorbed in the article when Natalie appeared.

"It's okay? I'm not disturbing you?"

"No, of course not."

"You looked like you were really concentrating."

"Yes, I was reading an article . . . on mozzarella trafficking."

This sent Natalie into gales of laughter, the kind you can have when you're tired. She couldn't stop. Markus understood how it could be funny and began to laugh as well. Inanity got a hold of them. All he'd done was answer without a second thought. And now she was laughing nonstop. It was an absolutely insane sight for Markus. Like looking at a fish with legs (to each his similes). For years, in hundreds of meetings, he'd seen a woman who was serious; sweet, yes, but always serious. He'd seen her smile, of course, and he'd even made her laugh before—but not like this. It was the first time that she laughed with such intensity. For her, it was all there: a moment that offered crystal-clear proof of what she liked experiencing with Markus. A man sitting in a café who gives you a big smile when you arrive and seriously announces he's reading an article on mozzarella trafficking.

Seventy-three

❖ ❖ ❖

Article from the Newspaper Métro, Entitled
"Mozzarella Racket Busted"

Five people were placed in police custody yesterday and the day before during a raid in Bondoufle (Essonne) targeting traffickers of "high-quality" mozzarella. According to Pierre Chuchkoff, the Évry squadron chief in charge of the investigation, "between 60 and 70 truck-bed pallets, totaling 33 tons, were stockpiled in two years" and resold in areas as far away as Villejuif (Val-de-Marne). This trafficking is not insignificant, considering the loss is estimated at 280,000 euros. The investigation, which began in June 2008 in response to a complaint from the Stef Group, was able to follow a trace that led to, among others, the managers of two pizzerias, one of which, located in Palaiseau, served as the hub. Police still have not discovered who was in charge of the operation or where the ill-gotten mozzarella gains have gone.

V.M.

Seventy-four

❖ ❖ ❖

During the course of a love affair, alcohol accompanies two op-posing moments: finding the other and the need to talk about it; and the time when there's no longer anything more to say to each other. They were in stage one. The stage where you don't notice time passing, where you recreate the story, especially the kissing scene. Natalie had thought the kiss had been motivated by a chance impulse. But maybe not? Maybe chance doesn't ex-ist. And all of it had only been the unconscious evolution of an intuition. The impression that she'd feel right with this man. This made her happy, then serious, then happy again. Swing-ing unremittingly from elation to sadness. And now the journey was leading her outside. To the cold. Natalie didn't feel very well. She'd caught cold with her goings and comings the night before. Where were she and Markus going? A kind of long walk was coming, because neither dared go to the other's place yet, and they certainly didn't want to separate. They let the feeling of indecision go on and on. And it's even more powerful at night.

"Can I kiss you?" he asked.

"I don't know . . . I'm starting to get a cold."

"Doesn't matter. I'm ready to be sick with you. Can I kiss you?"

———

Natalie had been so happy that he asked her the question. It was a form of sensitivity. Each moment with him went beyond the ordinary. After what she'd been through, how could she have imagined ever again entering a magical realm? There was something unique about the man.

She said yes with a movement of her head.

Seventy-five

❖ ❖ ❖

Dialogue from Woody Allen's Celebrity
That Inspired Markus's Reply

CHARLIZE THERON: You're not afraid of catching germs?
  And you know, I'm coming down with a cold and everything . . .
KENNETH BRANAGH: From you I'd be willing to catch ter-
  minal cancer.

Seventy-six

❖ ❖ ❖

Evenings can be extraordinary, nights unforgettable, and yet they always lead to mornings like all the others. Natalie was taking the elevator to her office. She hated ending up with someone in this cramped space, having to smile and exchange polite remarks, so she had waited for an empty car. She liked those several seconds as she rose toward her day, in that cage that transforms us into ants in a tunnel. She got out and found herself face to face with her boss. This is no idiom: they literally collided with each other.

"How surprising . . . I was telling myself that we don't see much of each other these days . . . and boom, there you are! If I'd known I had such power, I would have sent out another wish . . ."

"Clever of you."

"But seriously, I have to talk to you. Can you stop by and see me in a bit?"

Lately, Natalie had almost forgotten that Charles existed. He was like an old telephone number, an element that no longer jibes with the times. He was like a pneumatic mail tube, and they hadn't existed in Paris since 1983. She found it strange to have to go back to his office. How long ago had she stopped going there? She wasn't sure, exactly. The past was beginning to warp, to get diluted in hesitations, to hide under blotches of forgetfulness. And that was the happy proof that the present was resuming its role. She let most of the morning go by, then made up her mind.

Seventy-seven

❖   ❖   ❖

Examples of Telephone Numbers from Another Century

Odéon 32-40

*

Passy 22-12

*

Clichy 12-14

Seventy-eight

❖ ❖ ❖

Natalie walked into Charles's office. She immediately noticed that the shutters were less open than usual; it felt like an attempt to plunge the morning into darkness.

"It's true that it's been a long time since I've been here," she said as she walked in . . .

"Yes, a long time . . ."

"You must have read some dictionary definitions in the meantime . . ."

"Oh, that . . . no. I stopped. I'm sick of definitions. Frankly, can you tell me what use there is in knowing the meaning of words?"

"You wanted to see me to ask that?"

"No . . . no . . . we spend our time walking past each other . . . and I just wanted to know how you're doing . . . how it's going these days . . ."

He'd practically stammered these last words. Face to face with such a woman, he was a train derailed. He didn't understand why she had such an effect on him. She was beautiful, of course, had a way of dovetailing with his idea of the sublime, but still: was that enough? He was a powerful man, and sometimes

redheaded secretaries tittered as he went by. He could have had
women, he could have spent every day from five to seven in
five-star hotels. Then why hadn't he? He had no answer. He was
a slave to his first impression. It had to be that. The moment
he'd seen her face on her résumé, when he'd said, let me do the
interview with her. Then she'd appeared, young and married,
pale and indecisive, and a few seconds after, he'd offered her
some Krisprolls. Could he have fallen in love with a photo? Because nothing wears you out more than living under the sensual
dictates of beauty set in stone. He kept studying her. She didn't
want to sit down. She walked around the office, touching things,
smiling at some trifle: an intense incarnation of femininity. Finally, she walked around his desk and stood behind him.

"What . . . are you doing?"

"I'm looking at your head."

"But why?"

"I'm looking behind your head. Because I think you have an
idea at the back of your mind."

That's all he needed: some humor on her part. Charles was no
longer at all in control of the situation. She was behind him,
amused. For the first time, the past seemed really past. He'd
been in the dress circle during the dark days. He'd spent nights
thinking that she might commit suicide, and there she was now,
behind him, extremely alive.

"Come and sit down, please," he said calmly.

"All right."

"You seem happy. And it makes you look beautiful."

Natalie didn't answer. She was hoping that he hadn't asked

her to come so he could make some new admission. He went on, "You have nothing to tell me?"

"No, you're the one who wanted to see me."

"Everything is going well with your team?"

"Yes, I think so. Actually, you know better than I do. You have the figures."

"And with . . . Markus?"

So that was the idea in the back of his mind. He wanted to talk about Markus. How could she not have thought of it before?"

"I've heard you go out to dinner with him a lot."

"Who told you that?"

"Everything gets out in this place."

"So what? That's my private life. What's it have to do with you?" Suddenly Natalie stopped. Her face changed color. She looked at Charles, at how shabby he seemed, hanging on her words, lying in wait for an explanation, hoping more than anything for a denial. She kept watching him for a long time, without knowing what to do. Finally she decided to leave the office, without adding another word. She left her boss in his uncertainty, in his fine frustration. She hadn't been able to stand the gossip, people talking behind her back. She detested the entire routine: notions in the backs of their minds, words behind her back, shooting below the belt. It was the phrase "everything gets out" in particular that had bothered her. Now that she thought about it again, she could see it was true: yes, she'd sensed something in the eyes of others. Somebody having seen them at the restaurant, or simply leaving together, was enough to make the entire company go into action. Why was she getting excited?

She'd answered curtly that it was her life. She could have easily said to Charles, "Yes, I can see us becoming a man and a
woman." With conviction. But no, she didn't want to label the
situation, and it was out of the question for anyone at all to push
her into doing so. As she headed back to her office, she passed
some coworkers and noticed the change. The looks of compassion and sympathy were being eaten away by something else.
But she still couldn't imagine what was going to happen.

Seventy-nine

❖ ❖ ❖

Release Date of the Claude Lelouch Film
A Man and a Woman
With Anouk Aimée and Jean-Louis Trintignant

July 12, 1966

Eighty

❖ ❖ ❖

After Natalie left, Charles kept still for a long period of time. He understood perfectly how poorly he'd conducted that conversation. He'd been clumsy. In particular, he'd been incapable of telling her what he was really feeling, of saying, "Yes, it does have something to do with me. You didn't want to go out with me, because you didn't want to be with any man again. So, yes, I have the right to know what you're feeling. I have the right to know what you like about him, and what you don't like about me. You know very well how in love with you I was, how difficult it was for me. You owe me an explanation, that's all I'm asking." That's about what he would have wanted to say. But it's never like that: you're always five minutes behind when it comes to having a conversation about love.

He couldn't concentrate the rest of the day. When he'd set matters straight with Natalie, on that evening of so many ties in championship soccer, he'd come to terms with things. By some strange sexual logic, it had even led to reconnecting with his wife. They'd made love for weeks, finding each other through the medium of their bodies. You could even have called it a

magnificent time. There can be a lot more emotion in the redis-
covery of love than there is in its mere discovery. And then, the
agony had slowly resumed its course, like snickering; how could
they have believed they loved each other again? It had been a
passage, a parenthesis in the form of masked despair, a patch of
level terrain between two mountains of pathos.

Charles felt worn out, exhausted. He was sick of Sweden and
the Swedish. Of their taxing habit of always trying to stay calm.
Never shouting on the telephone. Their way of being Zen, pro-
viding employee massages. All this well-being was beginning to
grate on him. He missed Mediterranean hysteria, and he sometimes dreamed of doing business with carpet salesmen. This was
his frame of mind when he got the information about Natalie's
private life. Since then, he hadn't been able to stop thinking
about this Markus person. How had someone with such an idiotic first name been able to attract Natalie? He hadn't wanted to
believe it. He was in a good enough position to know that her
heart was sort of like the mirage of an oasis; as soon as you got
closer, it vanished. But this time was different. Her extravagant,
disproportionate reaction seemed to confirm the rumor. Oh no,
it couldn't be. He'd never be able to bear it. "How did it happen?" Charles kept repeating. The Swede must have cast a spell
on her, or something like that. Put her under, hypnotized her,
given her a potion to drink. It could only have been that. She'd
seemed so different. Yes, maybe that's what had hurt him the
most: she wasn't his Natalie anymore. Something had changed.
A bona fide modification. There was only one solution, then: call
in this Markus and see what he was made of. Discover his secret.

Eighty-one

❖ ❖ ❖

*Number of Languages, Including Swedish,
in Which You Can Read
Michel Butor's* La Modification (Second Thoughts),
Prix Renaudot, 1957

20

Eighty-two

❖ ❖ ❖

Markus had been raised with the notion that you must never make waves. That wherever you went, you must keep being discreet. Life was supposed to be like a passageway. So, when called in by the director, he was bound to panic. He could be a man, he could have a sense of humor and a sense of responsibility, he could be counted on; but as soon as it was a matter of relating to authority, he found himself becoming a child again. He was in turmoil, assailed by a host of questions. Why does he want to see me? What have I done? Did I do a bad job negotiating the insurance part of file 114? Have I gone to the dentist too often lately? Guilt besieged him from all sides. And maybe that was his true nature. The absurd feeling of punishment to come, hanging permanently over him like a sword of Damocles.

He knocked on the door his way, always with two fingers. Charles told him to enter.

"Hello, I'm here to see you . . . since you asked for . . ."

"I don't have the time right now . . . I have a meeting."

"Oh, fine then."

" . . . "

"Good, I'll leave then. I'll stop by later."

Charles dismissed the employee, because he didn't have time to see him. He was waiting for the famous Markus, without imagining for a second that he'd just seen him. The bastard had snared Natalie's heart, and now he had the nerve not to show up when he was called. What kind of rebel could he be? It wasn't going to happen like this. Who did he think he was? Charles telephoned his secretary.

"I asked a Markus Lundell to come and see me, and he still isn't here. Can you see what's going on?"

"But you asked him to leave."

"No, he didn't come."

"Yes, he did. I just saw him leaving your office."

Then Charles's mind went blank, as if wind had suddenly blown through his body. The wind of the north, undoubtedly. He almost fainted. He asked his secretary to call him back. Markus, who'd barely sat down on his chair, had to get up again. He wondered if his boss was having some fun with him. Perhaps he was irritated with the Swedish shareholders and was getting even using one of the employees who came from that country. Markus didn't want to be a yo-yo. If this kept up, he really was going to give in to pressure from Jean-Pierre, the union representative on the second floor.

He walked into Charles's office again. The latter's mouth was full. He was trying to calm down by eating a Krisprolls. We often try to relax with the help of things that get on our nerves. He was shaking, twitching, letting the crumbs fall from his mouth. Markus was dumbfounded. How could a man like that be in charge of a company? But the most dumbfounded was definitely Charles. How could a man like that be in charge of Natalie's heart? From the perplexity of both was born a moment hanging in time, in which neither could imagine what was going to happen next. Markus had no idea what to expect. And Charles didn't know what he was going to say. More than anything, he was in a deep state of shock. But how can it be possible? He's repulsive . . . he has no body to speak of . . . he's limp as a noodle, you can see it right off . . . oh no, it can't be . . . and then, he has this way of looking sideways at people . . . oh no, how horrible . . . not at all Natalie, this guy . . . nothing at all, no, no . . . oh it's disgusting . . . it's out of the question for him to keep hanging around her . . . out of the question . . . I'm going to send him back to Sweden . . . yes, that's it . . . a nice little transfer . . . I'm transferring him tomorrow!

Charles could have spun his gears like this for a very long time. He was incapable of speaking. But really, he'd called him in, so he had to say something. To gain some time, he offered, "Want a Krisprolls?"

"No thanks. I left Sweden to stop eating that kind of cracker . . . so I'm not going to start doing it again here."

"Ha . . . ha . . . very funny . . . ha . . . hee!"

Charles exploded into gales of laughter. The dickhead had a sense of humor. But what a dickhead . . . they're the worst, the ones who look depressed and surprise us with humor . . . you're not expecting it, and bam, a joke . . . That had to be his secret. Charles had always thought that was his weak point, that he hadn't made the women in his life laugh enough. He even wondered, thinking of his own wife, whether he wasn't gifted with a talent for making them gloomy. It's true that Laurence hadn't laughed for two years, three months, and seventeen days. He remembered, because he'd noted it in his calendar, the same way you keep track of the eclipses of the moon. "Today, my wife laughed." Still, he had to stop digressing. He should say something. What was he afraid of, after all? He was the boss. He was the one who decided on the totals for the lunch vouchers, which did amount to something, after all. No, really, he should get a grip. But how could he speak to this guy? How could he look him in the eye? Oh yes, the fact that he could touch Natalie was disgusting. The idea of his putting his lips on hers. What a sacrilege, what a violation! Oh Natalie. He'd always loved Natalie, it was obvious. We never get over our passions. He'd thought it would be easy to forget. But no, the feeling that had passed had only hibernated in him and was resurfacing now in its most cynical dimension.

He saw another solution, and it was more radical than a transfer: fire him. He had to have committed some professional violation. Everybody makes mistakes. But then, he wasn't everybody. His going out with Natalie was proof of that. Maybe he was a model employee, one of those who works overtime with a smile, who never asks for a raise—one of the worst, consequently. This genius might not even be in a union.

"You wanted to see me?" Markus tried to say, interrupting the long moments Charles had just spent in the apnea of shock.

"Yes . . . yes . . . I'm just finishing thinking about something, then I'm yours."

He couldn't make him wait like that. Or else, what if . . . he left him like that all day, just to see his reaction? But whatever strategy he used, it would work in some way. Because now that he thought of it—there's nothing more uncomfortable than to remain opposite someone who doesn't speak to you. Especially when it's your boss. And any other employee would have shown signs of anxiety, would have maybe sweated a few drops, made a gesture, crossed and uncrossed his legs . . . but this time, well, it wasn't the case. Markus had spent ten minutes, maybe fifteen, without moving. With perfect stoicism. It was unheard of, now that he thought about it again. This man had to be endowed with great mental strength.

At that moment, Markus was merely paralyzed by a very uncomfortable feeling of uncertainty. He didn't understand what was going on. For years, he'd never seen his boss, and now the man had summoned him to wrap him in silence. Each of them presented an image of strength to the eyes of the other, and neither was aware of it. It was up to Charles to speak first but—not a chance. His words were locked inside him. He was hypnotized, and kept looking right into Markus's eyes. At first he'd thought about getting rid of him, but a second possibility was occurring to him. It was obvious that, in conjunction with his hostility, a certain fascination was forming inside him. He was very far from wanting to turn him away; he had to see him at work. At last he began to speak to him.

"Sorry to have made you wait. It's just that I really prefer taking time to weigh my words when I'm speaking to someone. Especially when it's a matter of announcing what I have to say to you."

" . . . "

"The thing is, I've had wind of your management of file 114. You see, nothing escapes me here. I know everything. And I must say that I'm very happy to count you among us. And I've talked about you in Sweden, too, and they're very proud of having a countryman who is so efficient."

"Thanks . . ."

"But I'm the one who's thanking you. We feel you're a driving force in this company. What's more, I'd like to congratulate you personally. I think I'm not spending enough time with the good elements of this firm. I'd enjoy getting to know you better. Maybe we could go to dinner together, hmm? What do you think of that, hmm? Hmm, good idea, isn't it?"

"Er . . . okay."

"Oh, great, I'm so looking forward to it! Anyway, there's nothing but work in our lives . . . we'll be able to talk about lots of other things. I think it's good sometimes to break through the barrier between bosses and workers."

"If you say so."

"Well, then, tonight . . . Markus! Have a nice afternoon . . . and hurray for work!"

Markus left the office feeling as stunned as the sun during an eclipse.

Eighty-three

❖ ❖ ❖

Number of Packages of Krisprolls
Sold in 2002

22.5 million

Eighty-four

❖ ❖ ❖

The rumor spread throughout the company: Markus and Natalie were an item. The truth: they'd only kissed three times. The fantasy: she was pregnant. Yes, people embroidered. And to determine the extent of a piece of gossip, you only need to add up the visits to the coffee machine. Today, the number promised to be legendary. Although everybody in the company may have known Natalie, no one really knew who Markus was. He was an unobtrusive link in the chain, the basting thread for a garment. As he went back to his office, slightly stunned by what he'd just experienced, he felt a great many eyes on him. He didn't understand why. He stopped in the men's room to check for creases in his jacket, loose locks of hair, spaces between his teeth, and the color of his face. Nothing to do with any of that; everything was in place.

This focus on him kept growing as the day went on. A lot of employees found excuses to come and see him. They asked him questions, or said they'd come to the wrong door by mistake. Maybe it was just coincidence. One of those days incredibly full of events, without anyone really knowing why. It's the moon, his

Swedish aunt, who was famous in Norway as a fortune-teller, would have said. With all these interruptions, he hadn't really had time to work. That took the cake: he hadn't done a thing on the day his boss congratulated him. Maybe that's also what was getting in his way. Sudden encouragement isn't taken easily when you've never been in the dress circle before, when no one has ever noticed what you were doing. And then, there was Natalie. Always inside him. More and more. Their last date had given him a lot of confidence. Life was beginning to take a strange turn, gently moving past fears and uncertainties.

Natalie, too, had felt something stirring around her. It had only been a vague feeling until the moment when Chloé, an expert in confrontations, had dared ask, "Mind if I ask you a question?"

"Okay."

"Everybody is saying you're having an affair with Markus. Is it true?"

"I already told you that it has nothing to do with you."

This time, Natalie was really irritated. Everything she'd liked about that young girl seemed to have evaporated. All she saw in her now was a base obsession. She'd already been shocked by Charles's attitude, and now here it was again. What were they all getting so worked up about? Chloé went for broke and stammered out, "It's just that I can't at all imagine you . . ."

"That's enough. You can leave," said Natalie heatedly.

Instinctively, she felt that the more they criticized Markus, the more she'd feel close to him. That what was happening was forcing them closer together in a world that was far away from the incomprehension of others.

Chloé left the office, feeling like a stupid idiot. She so wanted to have a privileged relationship with Natalie and had gone about it like a fool. Nevertheless, she really was shocked. Didn't she have the right to express it? What's more, she wasn't the only one. There was something outlandish in the idea of those two being together. It wasn't that she didn't like Markus, nor even that she found him repugnant, it was just that she couldn't manage thinking of him with a woman. She'd always considered him a UFO from the world of men; whereas, in her eyes, Natalie had always represented a sort of feminine ideal. That is why their association disturbed her and instinctively pushed her to react. She was well aware that she'd been insensitive, but when everyone asked her, "So? So? Any information?" she figured her privileged position ought to hold some real weight.

Eighty-five

❖ ❖ ❖

Excuses Used by Employees
to Go and See Markus

I'd really like to take my wife on vacation
to Sweden this summer. Have any advice to give me?

*

Got an eraser?

*

Oh, sorry. I went to the wrong office.

*

Still working on 114?

*

Is your intranet working?

*

It really is a drag that your fellow Swede died
before he had the time to see the success of his trilogy.

Eighty-six

❖ ❖ ❖

In the middle of the afternoon, Natalie and Markus took a break together and met on the roof. It had become their refuge, their vault. As soon as their eyes met, they understood that something unusual was happening. That both of them had become targets for others' curiosity. They began to laugh at such idiocy and held each other close, the best way to create silence. Natalie murmured that she wanted to see him that evening and even wished that evening were now. It was beautiful, it was sweet, of an unexpected intensity. Markus was embarrassed, because he wasn't free. It was a dreadful quandary: he was beginning to consider every second without Natalie as meaningless, and yet he absolutely couldn't cancel dinner with his boss. Natalie was surprised and didn't dare ask what he had planned. She was particularly astonished to find herself suddenly in a weak position, the one who waits. Markus explained to her that he was having dinner with Charles.

"Tonight? He invited you to dinner?"

At that moment she didn't know whether she should laugh or be furious. Charles didn't have the right to have dinner with a member of her team without even informing her. She understood immediately that it had nothing to do with work. Up to now, Markus hadn't really been trying to dissect the reason for his boss's sudden interest. After all, it was plausible: he was doing a good job on 114.

"And did he say why he wanted to have dinner with you?"

"Um . . . yes . . . he wanted to congratulate me . . ."

"That doesn't seem weird to you? Do you think he has dinner with every employee he wants to congratulate?"

"You know, I found him so weird that nothing he does seems weird."

"That's for sure. You're right."

Natalie adored Markus's way of taking things. It could pass for naïveté, but it wasn't. There was something sweet about it in a childlike sense, a capacity for accepting situations, even the wackiest ones. He went up to her and kissed her. It was their fourth kiss, the most natural. At the beginning of a relationship, you can analyze almost every kiss. Everything stands out perfectly in a memory that advances slowly into the confusion of repetition. Natalie decided not to say a word about Charles and his grotesque motives. Markus would discover for himself what was hiding behind this dinner.

Eighty-seven

❖ ❖ ❖

Markus had gone quickly to his place to change because his get-together with his boss wasn't until nine o'clock. As was his habit, he wavered among several sports jackets. And opted for the most professional-looking one. The most serious, not to say the grimmest. He looked like an undertaker on vacation. Just when he needed to take the suburban train again there was a problem. Already, the passengers were beginning to get excited. They lacked information. Was it a fire? A suicide attempt? No one really knew. The panic reached Markus's car, and his first thought was that he was going to keep his boss waiting. Which was the case. Charles had been sitting there for more than ten minutes, drinking a glass of red wine. He was feeling annoyed, even very annoyed, because no one had ever kept him waiting like this. And certainly not an employee of whose very existence he'd been unaware that same morning. However, at the heart of the annoyance another feeling was born. The same feeling he'd experienced that morning, but this time it was coming back with more force. It had to do with a certain fascination. That guy was really capable of anything. Who would dare arrive late to a meeting like this? Who had the ability to fly in the face of authority like this? There was nothing else to say about it. This man deserved Natalie. It was undeniable. It was mathematical. It was chemical.

Sometimes, when you're late, you tell yourself that it won't help anything to run. You tell yourself that thirty-five minutes has exactly the same import as thirty. So you might as well add a little waiting to the other person's share of waiting, and avoid arriving in a sweat. This is what Markus decided. He didn't want to seem out of breath and red-faced. He knew it: as soon as he ran just a little, he looked like a newborn baby. So he left the subway terrified at the idea of being so late (and not having been able to apologize because he didn't have his boss's cell phone number), yet still walking. And that's how he appeared at his dinner, nearly an hour late, acting calm, very calm. The black sports jacket accentuated the spectral effect that bordered on the funereal. A little like a film noir in which the hero comes forth in silence from the shadows. Charles had almost finished a bottle of wine while waiting. It had made him romantic, nostalgic. He didn't even listen to Markus's excuses about the suburban train line. His arrival was grace incarnate.

And the evening would find its bearings on the triumph of that first impression.

Eighty-eight

❖ ❖ ❖

***Miss Teschmacher and Lex Luthor Discussing Superman
in the Movie* Superman *(1978)***

MISS TESCHMACHER: Lex, what's the story on this guy? Do
you think it's the genuine article?

LEX LUTHOR: If he is, he's not from this world.

MISS TESCHMACHER: Why?

LEX LUTHOR: Because, if any human being were going to
perpetrate such a fantastic hoax, it would have been me!

Eighty-nine

❀ ❀ ❀

During the entire dinner, Markus was astounded by Charles's behavior. The latter babbled, blabbed, bumbled. He was incapable of finishing a sentence. Flew into sudden bursts of laughter, but never at the moment when Markus was trying to be funny. He was like somebody with jet lag in relation to the present moment. After a while, Markus dared to ask, "Are you all right?"

"All right? Me? You know, since yesterday, constantly. Especially right now."

The incoherence of that answer confirmed Markus's suspicions. Charles hadn't gone completely insane. He was quite aware, during rare flashes of lucidity, that he was losing his marbles. But he couldn't get hold of himself. He was suffering from some kind of short circuit. The Swede sitting opposite him had turned his life, his system upside down. He was struggling to return to reality. As for Markus, although his past was far from eventful, he was close to thinking that this dinner was the most ghastly one of his life. And when it came to ghastly, he was well versed. However, he couldn't refrain from beginning to feel compassion, the desire to help this man who was going to the dogs.

"Can I do something for you?"

"Yes, definitely, Markus . . . I'm going to think about it, that's nice. Now, it's true, you are nice . . . it shows . . . in your way of looking at me . . . you're not judging . . . I understand everything . . . I understand everything, now . . ."

"You understand what?"

"But I understand for Natalie. The more I see you, the more I understand everything I'm not."

Markus put down his glass. He'd started to suspect that all of this could have something to do with Natalie. Contrary to all expectations, his first feeling was one of relief. It was the first time that someone had talked to him about her. At that precise moment, Natalie was disengaged from fantasy. She entered into the real part of his life.

Charles went on. "I love her. Did you know that I love her?"

"I definitely think you've had too much to drink."

"So? Being drunk won't change anything. I'm still lucid, very much so. Lucid about everything I'm not. Looking at you, I realize the point to which I've wasted my life . . . the point to which my life hasn't stopped being trivial, and a permanent compromise . . . it will seem crazy to you, but I'm going to tell you something I've never told a soul: I wanted to be an artist . . . yes, I know, same old song . . . but really, when I was little, I adored painting little boats . . . it was pure bliss . . . I have a whole collection of miniature gondolas . . . I put hours into painting them . . . into being so precise with every detail . . . how I would have loved to keep painting . . . to live my life in that kind of frenzied calm . . . and instead of that, I'm stuffing myself with Krisprolls throughout the day . . . and those days go on forever . . . they're about as different from one another as the Chinese are . . . and my sex life . . . my wife . . . all that stuff . . . I don't even want to talk about it . . . I realize all of it now . . . I see you, and I realize . . ."

Suddenly Charles interrupted his monologue. Markus was uncomfortable. It's never easy when a person you don't know starts confiding in you, and even less easy when it happens to be your boss. All he had left was humor to try to lighten up the atmosphere.

"You saw all that by looking at me? That's really the effect I have on you? In such a short time . . ."

"And on top of that, you have a great sense of humor. You're a genius, really. There was Marx, there was Einstein, and now there's you."

Markus couldn't find a rejoinder to that rather excessive remark. Luckily, the waiter appeared.

"Have you decided?"

"Yes, I'll have the beef," said Charles. "Very rare."

"The fish for me."

"Very good, gentlemen," said the waiter as he left.

He was barely six feet away when Charles called him back. "Actually, I'll have the same as the gentleman. The fish for me, too."

"Very good, got it," said the waiter, leaving again.

After a silence, Charles admitted, "I decided to do everything like you."

"Do everything like me?"

"Yes, kind of like with a mentor."

"You know, there's not a lot to do to be like me."

"I don't agree. For example, your sports jacket. I think it would be a good idea if I had the same one. I ought to wear the same clothes as you. You have a unique style. Everything is thought out; it shows that you leave nothing to chance. And the same for women. Right, and the same for that, right?"

"Uh, yes, I don't know. I can lend it to you if you want."

"There you go! That's so you: niceness personified. I say that I like your sports jacket, and in a second you offer to lend it to me. That is so wonderful. I realize I haven't lent out my sports jackets enough. All my life I've been a tremendously selfish person when it comes to sports jackets."

Markus realized that anything he'd say was bound to be inspired. The man opposite him was looking through a filter of admiration, if not of veneration. Continuing his inquiry, Charles asked, "Tell me more about you."

"To tell you the truth, I don't often think about who I am."

"There you go! That's it! My problem is that I think too much. I'm always wondering what others think. I ought to be more stoic."

"For that you'd have to be born in Sweden."

"Ha! Very funny! You need to teach me to be funny like that. What a sense of repartee! Here's to you! Can I pour you some more?"

"No, I think I've had enough."

"And what a sense of control! Okay, that one I think I won't do like you. I'm allowing myself one infraction."

The waiter arrived with the two fish and wished them bon appétit. They began to eat. Suddenly, Charles raised his head from his plate.

"What an idiot I am. All of this is ridiculous."

"What?"

"I hate fish."

"Oh . . ."

"But, it's worse than that."

"Oh really?"

"Yes, I'm allergic to fish."

" . . . "

"It's all been said now. I'll never be able to be like you. I can never be with Natalie. All that because of fish."

Ninety

❖ ❖ ❖

Some Technical Details Concerning
Allergies to Fish

Allergy to fish isn't rare. It's one of the "Big Eight" allergies. For those who fall victim to it, the main issue is knowing whether it's an allergy to only one kind of fish or several. Clinically, half those patients allergic to one type of fish are also allergic to others. That makes it necessary to do skin tests for allergic cross-reactivity and sometimes to do provocation tests (using the food in question) for cases in which skin tests aren't sufficient. One might also wish to know whether certain fish are less likely to cause allergic reactions than others. To answer this question, a research team compared cross-reactivity among nine species of fish: fresh or salted cod, salmon, whiting, mackerel, tuna, herring, bass, halibut, and plaice. Results showed that the tuna and the mackerel (both belonging to the Scombridae family) are better tolerated and that halibut and plaice come in second. Contrarily, the cod, salmon, whiting, herring, and bass indicated strong cross-reactivities, meaning that if you're allergic to one of them, you have a better chance of being allergic to the others.

Ninety-one

❖   ❖   ❖

After the revelation about fish, the dinner was plunged into a realm of silence. Markus tried several times to revive the conversation, but in vain. Charles didn't eat anything and contented himself with drinking. They looked like an old couple who no longer have anything to say to each other. Which gives them permission to drift into a kind of deep thought. Time passes amiably (and so, sometimes, do years).

Once outside, Markus had to rein in his boss. He couldn't drive in that condition. He wanted him to climb into a taxi, as fast as possible. He was in a hurry to finish with the ordeal of the evening. But—bad news—the fresh air perked Charles up. He wanted to get going again, take a walk.

"Don't leave me, Markus. I still want to talk to you."

"But you haven't said a word for an hour. And you've had too much to drink. Better to go home."

"Oh, enough with the serious act for a while! You're really wearing me out! We'll have one last drink, and that's it. That's an order!"

Markus didn't have a choice.

They ended up in the sort of place where people of a certain age brush against each other lasciviously. It wasn't in the strictest sense a dance club, but it looked like one. Sitting on a pink banquette, they ordered two herbal teas. Behind them reared a hasty lithograph, kind of a *nature morte*, but one that was very dead. Charles seemed calmer now. Spiraling into a depression once again. Weariness flooded his face. When he thought about the years that had gone by, he remembered Natalie's return to work after her tragedy. He was haunted by a vision of that damaged woman. What makes a detail, a gesture, leave such a deep mark on us, turning an insignificant moment into the central focus of a stretch of time? Natalie's face eclipsed his memories, career, family life. He could write a book on the subject of Natalie's knees, whereas he was incapable of citing his daughter's favorite singer. At the time, he'd made up a reason for himself. He understood that she wasn't ready for a new experience. But, deep down, he hadn't stopped hoping. Today, everything seemed without interest to him: life was grim. He felt suffocated. The Swedes were tense because of the financial crisis. The country had been on the edge of bankruptcy and that had undermined quite a few certainties. He also sensed a building hate for the bosses. Like other managers, he might have to cut himself off from the next industrial dispute. And then there was his wife. She didn't understand him. They talked about money so often that sometimes he confused her with his creditors. Everything blended into a colorless world, where even femininity itself was a vestige, and no one took the time anymore to produce the sound of spike heels. The silence of every day announced a silence of always. That is why he was losing his footing at the idea of Natalie with another man . . .

———

He brought up all of it with a lot of sincerity. Markus understood that he had to talk about Natalie. A woman's name, and
the night seemed boundless. But what could he say about her?
He barely knew her. He would simply have to admit, "You're
mistaken . . . we aren't really together . . . right now all it's been
is two, three, or four kisses . . . and I'm not even explaining how
weird it all is . . ." but no sound came out of his mouth. He had
trouble talking about her, he realized now. His boss had put his
head on his shoulder and was pushing him into being candid.
So in turn Markus forced himself to tell his version of his life
with Natalie. His analysis of all his Natalian moments. Without
expecting it, he was suddenly bombarded by throngs of memories. Fleeting moments that already reached far into the past,
well before the impulse of the kiss.

There was the first time. He'd had his job interview with her.
He'd immediately told himself, "I could never work with a
woman like that." He hadn't come off well, but Natalie had instructions to hire a Swede. Markus was there then because of
some business about a quota. He'd never known it. His first
impression of her had stuck in his mind for months. Now he
thought again about that way she had of pushing her locks of
hair behind her ear. It was that action that had fascinated him.
During team meetings he'd hoped she'd do it again, but no, it
had been a single moment of magic. He also thought of other
gestures, such as when she placed her files at the corner of the
table, or her way of rapidly wetting her lips before drinking, or
the time she took for breath between two sentences, and the way

she had of sometimes pronouncing *s*, especially at the end of the day, and her smile of politeness, or thanks, and her spike heels, oh yes her spike heels that set off her calves to such advantage. He detested the wall-to-wall carpeting at the company, and had even asked one day, "But who could have invented the wall-to-wall carpet?" And so many things, more and more. Yes, it was all coming back to him now, and Markus realized that, inside, he'd accumulated a lot of fascination for Natalie. Every day near her had been the huge but surreptitious conquest of a veritable empire of the heart.

How long had he talked about her? He didn't know. Turning his head, he noticed that Charles had dozed off. Like a child who falls asleep listening to a story. To keep him from catching cold, with a sensitive gesture of attention, he covered him with his jacket. In the newfound silence, he studied the man about whose power he'd fantasized. Markus, who had so often felt as if he were living underwater, breathing through a snorkel, who'd so often envied others' lives, now realized that he wasn't the most unhappy. That even his routine pleased him. He was hoping to be with Natalie but, if that weren't the case, he wouldn't fall apart. Overwrought or fragile at moments as he could be, Markus had a certain strength. A sort of stability, calm. Something allowed him not to endanger his days. What good did it do to get in a flap when everything is absurd? he sometimes told himself, when he was obviously overnourished on Cioran's writings. Life can be beautiful when you understand the inconvenience of being born. The sight of Charles asleep reinforced this feeling of assurance, which was going to become even stronger in him.

———

Two women about fifty approached them to try to start a conversation, but Markus made a sign telling them not to make any noise. Although this was, after all, a place with music. At any rate, Charles straightened up, surprised to be opening his eyes in this pink cocoon. He saw Markus's face watching him and noticed the sports jacket that had been put on him. He smiled, and this slight movement of his face reminded him that he had a headache. It was time to leave. It was already early morning. And it was together that they arrived at the office. As they left the elevator, they separated with a handshake.

Ninety-two

❖ ❖ ❖

A little later that morning, Markus headed for the coffee machine. He immediately noticed employees stepping out of his
way as he walked by. He was Moses before the Red Sea. This
metaphor may appear exaggerated. But it's necessary to understand what was taking place. Markus, an employee who was as
unobtrusive as he was lackluster, who'd often been worthy of
the word nondescript, had ended up in less than a day going out
with one of the most beautiful women in the company, if not
the most beautiful (and to give full credit to such an achievement, it was a woman reputed to be stone cold when it came to
flirting), and had also gone to dinner with the boss. He and the
boss had even been seen arriving together that morning, which
was enough to feed malicious gossip. This was a lot for one man.
Everybody greeted him, hitting him up with, "How's it goin'?"
and, "Is file 114 coming along?" Suddenly they were interested
in that damned file, in its slightest nuance of phrasing. So much
so that Markus, by the middle of the morning, came close to
being sick. Added to an all-nighter, the change was too brutal.
It was as if years of unpopularity were suddenly made up for,
condensed into a few minutes. Of course, all of that couldn't

be normal. There had to be a reason, something shady. People said he was a mole working for Sweden, or the son of the biggest shareholder; they said he was gravely ill; they said he was very well known in his country as a porn actor; they said he'd been chosen to represent mankind on Mars; they also said he was a close friend of Natalie Portman.

Ninety-three

Oprah Winfrey's Announcement
to Barbara Walters on ABC,
December 8, 2010

"I'm not even kind of a lesbian. And the reason why [the rumor] irritates me is because it means that somebody must think I'm lying."

Ninety-four

❖ ❖ ❖

Natalie and Markus met for lunch. He was tired, but his eyes were still wide open. She couldn't get over hearing that the dinner had lasted all night. Maybe things always happened that way with him? Maybe nothing happened in the way it was anticipated. She would have wanted to laugh about it. But she didn't at all like what she was seeing. She felt tense, irritated by the agitation around them. It sent her back to the meanness of some people after François's funeral. To the inhibiting expressions of compassion. Maybe it was a half-baked comparison. But in it she saw vestiges of the times of the collaboration. As she observed certain reactions, she'd say to herself, "If there were a new war, everything would be exactly the same." Perhaps this feeling was exaggerated, but the swiftness of rumor, allied with a certain spite, inspired disgust in her that was an echo of that dubious period.

She didn't understand why her affair with Markus was so interesting. Was it because of him? Because of what he gave off? Is that how pairings that lack rationality are seen? But it was ridiculous: is there anything less logical than an attraction?

Since her last discussion with Chloé, Natalie's anger hadn't subsided. Who did they all think they were? She reinterpreted brief glances from everyone as attacks.

"We've barely kissed, and I get the impression that everyone hates me now," she said.

"And everyone adores me!"

"Now that's clever, isn't it . . ."

"Just say the hell with it. Look at the menu. That's what counts. You want endives with Roquefort or the soup of the day as an appetizer? That's all that matters."

He certainly was right. However, she couldn't relax. She didn't understand why she was having such a strong reaction. Maybe she needed some time to understand that it was all connected to the rebirth of her emotions. It was a giddy sensation that she was transforming into aggression. Against all of them, and above all, against Charles.

"You know, the more I think about it, the more I tell myself that Charles's reaction is disgraceful."

"I think he loves you, that's all."

"That's no reason to play the clown with you."

"Calm down, it isn't that serious."

"I can't calm down, I can't . . ."

Natalie announced that she was going to see Charles after lunch so that he'd stop with the dramatics. Markus chose not to hinder her determination. He left room for a bit of silence, which she broke off with a confession. "Sorry, I'm on edge . . ."

"It's no big deal. Besides, you know news changes quickly . . . and two days from now they won't be talking about us anymore . . . there's a new secretary who just arrived, and I think Berthier's attracted to her . . . so you see . . ."

"That's no scoop. He jumps on everything that moves."

"Yes, true. But this is different. Remember he just got married to the accountant . . . so we're not safe from a little soap opera."

"More than anything I think I'm lost."

She'd spoken the sentence abruptly. Without the slightest transition. Instinctively, Markus took the soft part of the bread and started to crumble it in his hand.

"What are you doing?" Natalie asked him.

"I'm doing what they did in *Tom Thumb*. If you're lost, you've got to leave a trail of crumbs behind you as you go. That way, you can find your way back."

"Which leads me here . . . to you, I suppose?"

"Yes. Unless I'm hungry, and decide to eat the crumbs while I'm waiting for you."

Ninety-five

❀ ❀ ❀

Which Appetizer Natalie Chose
at Lunch with Markus

Soup of the day.*

---

* We haven't been able to obtain any details regarding the exact nature of that soup.

Ninety-six

✵　✵　✵

Charles was no longer at all the same man who'd passed the night with Markus. Halfway through the morning, he'd recovered his spirits and regretted his behavior. He was still wondering why he'd lost his footing at the sight of the Swede. Maybe he wasn't totally fulfilled and suffered from a variety of anxieties, but that was no reason for reacting like that. Especially in front of somebody. He was ashamed. It was going to push him into drastic behavior. Just like a lover can prove to be aggressive after a far from stellar sexual performance. He felt all the fragments of combat coalescing in him again. He began to do a few push-ups, but at that very moment, Natalie came into his office. He got up.

"You could have knocked," he said curtly.

She walked toward him the same way she'd walked toward Markus to kiss him. But this time it was to deliver a slap.

"There, I did it."

"But you can't do that! I can fire you for that."

Charles brought a hand to his face. And tremblingly repeated his threat.

"And I can attack you for harassment. You want me to show you the e-mails you sent me?"

"But why are you talking to me like that? I've always re-spected you."

"Yes, that's it. Put on your little act for me. All you wanted to do was sleep with me."

"I honestly don't understand you."

"Well, I don't understand what you went and did with Markus."

"Don't I have the right to have dinner with an employee?"

"Yes, okay, that's enough! Understand?" she shouted.

This did her a world of good, and she would have wanted to fly into an even bigger rage. Her reaction was excessive. By defend-ing her territory with Markus like that, she was betraying her confusion. The confusion she was always incapable of defining. Dictionaries stop where the heart starts. And maybe that's why Charles had stopped reading definitions when Natalie returned to work. There was nothing to say beyond giving voice to primal reactions.

As she was about to leave the office, Charles declared, "I had dinner with him because I wanted to get to know him . . . to know how you could have chosen a man that ugly, that insignifi-cant. I can understand your rejecting me, but that's something, you see, I'll never understand . . ."

"Shut up!"

"I you think I'm going to leave things just as they are. I've just been with the stockholders. Any moment now, your dear Markus is going to get a very important offer. An offer he'd be suicidal to refuse. Just one small problem: the job is in

Stockholm. But with the benefits he'll get, I think he won't hesitate long."

"You're pathetic. Especially since nothing can prevent me from resigning and going with him."

"You can't do that! I forbid it!"

"You're a pain, you really are . . ."

"And you can't do that to François, either!"

Natalie stared at him. Immediately he wanted to apologize for what he'd said; he knew he'd gone too far. But he couldn't move a muscle. Neither could she. That last sentence had knocked the life out of them. Finally, she left Charles's office, slowly, without saying anything. He sat there alone, certain of having lost her forever. Then he walked to the window to gaze out into empty space, intensely tempted.

Ninety-seven

❖ ❖ ❖

Once she was back sitting at her desk, Natalie consulted her calendar. She called Chloé to ask her to cancel all her meetings.

"But it isn't possible! You have to head the committee in an hour."

"Yes, I know," interrupted Natalie. "Okay, good, I'll call later."

She hung up, not knowing what to do. It was an important meeting, and she'd spent a lot of time preparing for it. But it was obvious that she could no longer work in this company after what had just happened. She remembered the first time she'd come to this building. She was still a young girl. She recalled those beginnings, François's advice. Perhaps that's what had been the hardest thing about his death. The sudden, brutal absence of their discussions. The end of those moments when you talked about each other's life, when you commented on it. She was finding herself alone at the edge of the abyss and deeply understood that her fragility was degrading her. That for three years she'd been putting on the most pathetic act there is. That deep down she had never been persuaded she wanted to live. She still felt so much guilt, so much ridiculous guilt when she returned again to the memory of the Sunday her husband had died. She should have held him back, kept him from going running. Wasn't that a wife's role? See to it that men stop running. She should have held him back, kissed him, loved him. She should have set down her book, interrupted her reading instead of letting him smash his life to pieces.

Her anger had subsided now. She gazed at her desk a moment more, then threw a few belongings into her bag. She turned off her computer, tidied up the drawers, and left. She was glad she didn't pass anyone, didn't have to say a word. Her escape had to be a silent one. She took a taxi, told the driver to go to the Saint-Lazare railroad station, and bought a ticket. As the train was leaving, she began to weep.

Ninety-eight

❖ ❖ ❖

Schedule of the Paris–Lisieux Train
Taken by Natalie

Departure: 4:33 p.m. Paris/Saint-Lazare
Arrival: 6:02 p.m. Lisieux

Ninety-nine

❁ ❁ ❁

Natalie's disappearance immediately jammed the functioning of every floor. She was supposed to preside over the most important meeting of the quarter. She'd left without giving the slightest instruction, hadn't notified anyone. In the hallways, some were rankled and criticized her lack of professionalism. In a few minutes, her reputation took a nosedive: the authority of the present over a reputation acquired in the course of years. Since everyone was aware of her connection to Markus, they continually went to see him. "Do you know where she could be?" He had to admit that he didn't. And that amounted almost to saying, "No, I have no particular connection to her. She doesn't share her wanderings with me." It was hard to have to express his lack of responsibility for the situation like that. This new episode was going to strip him of the prestige he'd accumulated the day before. It was as if they were suddenly remembering that he wasn't as important as all that. And people began to wonder how they could have thought—even only for an instant—that he was close to Natalie Portman.

——

He'd tried to reach her several times. To no avail. Her telephone was turned off. He couldn't work. He walked in circles. This was accomplished very quickly, given the size of his narrow office. What could he do? The confidence of the last few days was disintegrating rapidly. Their lunch together played in a loop in his head. "What counts is knowing what appetizer you're going to have." He remembered having said something like that. How was it possible to speak that way? It wasn't necessary to look for an answer. He hadn't been at his best. She'd said, hadn't she, that she was lost; and perched on his cloud, he'd been capable of nothing more than offering her a few superficial phrases. *Tom Thumb*! In what world was he living? Certainly not a world where women left you their address before running away. It was so obvious that everything was his fault. He made women run away. She was probably even going to become a nun. Taking trains and planes to get out of the air he breathed. He felt sick. Sick for having acted so poorly. The emotion of love is the mea culpa of emotions. You may end up thinking that the other's hurt all comes from you. You may think—mad as it always is— that some demiurgic movement has placed you right at the heart of the heart of the other. That life comes down to a bell jar of pulmonary valves. Markus's world was Natalie's. It was an entire, all-embracing world where he was simultaneously responsible for everything and for less than nothing.

And the ordinary world was coming back to him. Slowly, he managed to regain control of his mind. To balance white and black. He thought again of all the affection of their moments together. That truly genuine affection that couldn't die away like this. The fear of losing Natalie had clouded his mind. His anxiety was his vulnerability, that same vulnerability that could also be where his powers of attraction lay. By linking vulnerabilities, you reach a kind of strength. He didn't know what to do, no longer wanted to work, no longer thought about his day in a rational way. He wanted to be crazy, to run away, too, to take a taxi and board the first train that came along.

One Hundred

❖ ❖ ❖

Then he was called to the director of human resources. Obviously, everybody wanted to see him. He went there without the slightest apprehension. He had gotten over any fear of authority. Everything had been nothing but a ploy for several days. Mr. Bonivent welcomed him with a big smile. Immediately Markus thought, This smile is really a murder. It's essential for a director of human resources to look as though he's as concerned about the career of an employee as he'd be if it were a question of his own life. Markus noticed that Bonivent was worthy of his post.

"Oh, Mr. Lundell . . . what a pleasure to see you. I've been keeping my eye on you for some time, you know . . ."

"Really?" he answered, certain (and rightly so) that this man had just discovered his existence.

"Of course . . . everyone's career counts for me . . . and I must even admit that I have a genuine affection for you. Your way of never making any waves, never asking for anything. It's very unpretentious, and if I wasn't somewhat conscientious, well, I wouldn't have noticed your presence at the heart of our company . . ."

"Oh . . ."

"You're the employee that every employer dreams of."

"That's nice. Could you tell me why you wanted to see me?"

"Oh, that's so like you! Efficiency! Efficiency! We don't lose any time! If only everybody was like you!"

"So?"

"Fine . . . I'm going to be frank with you about the situation: management is offering you a job as team leader. With a significant pay raise, as goes without saying. You're an essential part of the strategic repositioning of our company . . . and I must say I'm not unhappy with this promotion . . . because there was a moment when I actively supported it."

"Thank you . . . I don't know what to say."

"Well, of course, we'll facilitate all the administrative steps necessary for the transfer."

"The transfer?"

"Yes. The job is in Stockholm. Where you're from!"

"But my going back to Sweden is out of the question. I'd rather go to the unemployment office than to Sweden."

"But . . ."

"There is no but."

"But yes there is. I don't think you have a choice."

Markus didn't bother answering and left the office without another word.

One Hundred One

The Circle of Contradictions

Created in late 2003 with the objective of introducing the NADHR* to HR professionals, the Circle of Contradictions brings together DHRs once a month at the Institute of Human Resources to discuss issues that concern those DHRs who must deal with the very crux of company paradoxes. These monthly meetings strive to be intelligently iconoclastic; sensitive subjects are dealt with in a professional if offbeat tenor. Humor is welcome, but officialese mumbo-jumbo is not![†]

---

* National Association of Directors of Human Resources.

[†] Subject for Thursday, January 13, 2009: "Thankfulness in a Time of Crisis: Priority to the Individual or to the Collective?" 6:30 p.m.–8:30 p.m., NADHR, 91 rue de Miromesnil, 75008 Paris.

One Hundred Two

❖   ❖   ❖

Usually Markus took his time walking through the hallways. He'd always considered these movements from one place to another as breaks. He was perfectly capable of getting up and saying, "I'm going to stretch my legs," in the same way others would go out for a cigarette. But by that point he was finished with all that. He charged. It was so strange to see him coming forward like that, as if propelled by rage. He was a souped-up diesel-engine car. There really was something souped-up about him: some sensitive chords had been struck, and they went straight to the heart.

He burst into his boss's office. Charles looked hard at his employee and instinctively placed his hand to his cheek. Markus stood stock still in the middle of the room, holding back his rage. Charles dared to say, "You know where she is?"

"No, I don't. All of you must stop asking me where Natalie is. I don't know."

"I just spoke to the clients on the telephone. They're furious. I can't get over the fact that she could do that to us!"

"I understand her perfectly."

"What do you want with me?"

"I'd like to tell you two things."

"Quickly. I'm in a hurry."

"The first is that I refuse your offer. How low of you. I don't know how you're going to look at yourself in the mirror anymore."

"Who told you I look at myself?"

"Fine, I don't care what the hell you do or don't do."

"And the second?"

"I quit."

Charles was stupefied by the man's speed of reaction. He hadn't hesitated an instant. He was refusing the offer and leaving the company. How could Charles have handled the situation so badly? And yet, no. Perhaps it was what he wanted? Seeing both of them run off with their unfortunate affair. Charles kept looking at Markus and couldn't read anything on his face. Because there was a kind of frozen rage on it. Which annihilated any readable expression. However, Markus had begun to walk toward him, slowly, with a confidence that was out of proportion. As if motivated by some unknown force. So strong that Charles couldn't avoid feeling afraid, very afraid.

"Now that you're not my boss anymore . . . I can . . ."

Markus didn't finish his sentence; his fist finished it for him. It was the first time he'd hit anyone. And he regretted not having done it before. Having looked for words to handle situations too many times.

"You can't do that! You're insane!" shouted Charles.

Markus came toward him again, made as if to hit him again. Charles reared back, terrified. He sat down in a corner of his office. And he stayed down in that position long after Markus left.

One Hundred Three

❖ ❖ ❖

October 29, 1960 in the Life of Muhammad Ali

In Louisville, he won his first professional fight, based on points, against Tunney Hunsaker.

One Hundred Four

❖ ❖ ❖

When she arrived at the Lisieux station, Natalie rented a car. She hadn't driven in a very long time. She was worried that she'd lost the automatic reflexes. The weather wasn't helping; it was beginning to rain. But she was filled with such intense weariness that for the moment nothing could frighten her. She drove faster and faster on small roads, saying bonjour to sadness. The rain interfered with her vision; at moments, she couldn't see anything.

That's when something happened. In the flash of a second, just that way, as she drove on. She saw the scene of the kiss with Markus again. At the moment the image appeared, she hadn't been thinking of him. Far from it. The vision suddenly forced itself into her consciousness. She began to think about the moments she'd spent with him. As she continued to drive, she began to regret leaving without saying a word to him. She didn't know why she hadn't thought of it. Her escape had been so rapid. It certainly was the first time she'd left the office that way. She knew she'd never go back to it, that a part of her life was over now. It was time to drive. However, she decided to stop at a service station. She got out of the car and looked around her. She didn't recognize anything. She'd probably made a wrong turn. Night was falling, it was deserted. And the rain completed this classic triptych of the imagery of despair. She sent a message to Markus. Just to tell him where she was. Two minutes later, she got the following answer: "I'm taking the first train for Lisieux. So much the better if it pleases you." Then a second message immediately after: "And what's more, it almost rhymes."

One Hundred Five

❀   ❀   ❀

Excerpt from "The Kiss," a Story
by Guy de Maupassant

Do you know the real source of our strength? The kiss, the kiss alone! . . . The kiss is only a preface, however . . .

One Hundred Six

❖ ❖ ❖

Markus got off the train. He, too, had left without telling any-one. They were going to find each other again, like two fugitives. He saw her, standing stock-still, at the other side of the station concourse. He began to walk toward her, slowly, sort of like in a movie. You'd have no trouble imagining the music that accom-panied this moment. Or else silence. Yes, silence would be good. You'd only hear their breathing. You'd almost be able to forget the sadness of the décor. Salvador Dalí would never have been able to be inspired by the Lisieux train station. It was empty and cold. Markus spotted a poster advertising the museum devoted to Thérèse de Lisieux. As he walked toward Natalie, he thought, "Hmm, strange, I always though that Lisieux was her last name . . ." Yes, that's really what he was thinking. And there was Nata-lie, so close to him. With those lips of the kiss. But her face was shut down. Her face was the Lisieux train station.

They went to the car. Natalie climbed into the driver's seat, and Markus rode shotgun. She started off. They hadn't said a word to each other yet. They looked like those teenagers who don't know what to say to each other on the first date. Markus had no idea where they were, no idea where they were going. He was following Natalie, and that was enough. After a moment, unable to stand the emptiness, he decided to turn on the radio. It was tuned to the oldies station. Alain Souchon's "L'amour en fuite" ("Love on the Run") reverberated through the car.

"Oh, it's incredible!" said Natalie.

"What?"

"This song. It's crazy. It's my song. And there . . . just like that."

Markus looked fondly at the radio. This contraption had let him renew his dialogue with Natalie. She was still saying how strange and crazy it was. That it was a sign. What kind of sign? That, Markus couldn't know. He was surprised at the effect this song had on his companion. But he was familiar with the strange facts of life, with strokes of luck, coincidences. The evidence that made you doubt rationality. At the end of that piece of music, she asked Markus to turn off the radio. She wanted to stay suspended in that song she'd always loved so much. Which she'd discovered in the last installment of the film series *The Adventures of Antoine Doinel*. She'd been born during that period, and maybe it was a complex feeling to define, but she felt she'd come from that moment. As if she were a product of that melody. Her sweet, sometimes melancholy personality, its lightness, all of it was absolutely 1978. It was her song, it was her life. And she couldn't get over such a stroke of luck.

She pulled over at the edge of the road. The darkness prevented Markus from seeing where they were. They got out. Then he made out some big metal bars, those at the entrance to a cemetery.

Next he discovered that they weren't big—they were immense. The same kind you'd find in front of a prison. Certainly the dead are condemned to perpetuity, but it's hard to imagine them trying to escape. Finally Natalie started to speak.

"François is buried there. He spent his childhood in this region."

" . . . "

"Of course, he never said anything to me. He didn't think he was going to die . . . but I know he wanted to be here . . . near the place where he'd grown up."

"I understand," murmured Markus.

"You know, it's funny, but I spent my childhood here, too. When François and I met, we thought it was a crazy coincidence. We could have run into each other hundreds of times during our adolescence, but we never saw each other. And it was in Paris that we met. Which just goes to show you . . . when you're supposed to meet somebody . . ."

Natalie stopped with that phrase. But the phrase kept going on inside Markus's mind. Whom was she talking about? About François, of course. About him, too, maybe? The double reading of the remark brought the symbolic nature of the situation into focus. It had a rare intensity. There they were, the two of them, side by side, just a few feet away from François's grave. Just a few feet away from a past that never finished finishing. So much rain fell on Natalie's face that you couldn't tell where the tears began. Markus saw them. He knew how to interpret the tears. Natalie's tears. He went to her and held her tight in his arms, as if he were encircling her suffering.

One Hundred Seven

❖　❖　❖

Second Part of "L'amour en fuite" ("Love on the Run"),
by Alain Souchon,
Heard by Markus and Natalie in the Car

You, me, we just couldn't cope.
Boohoo, tears without hope.
Leavin' each other, and both of us are mum.
It's love on the run,
Love on the run.

While I was sleeping,
a kid on the pillow.
We flew back and forth,
just like a swallow.
I moved in, then left our two rooms and kitchen,
Named the kid Colette, Gregory, or Christian.

Spent my whole life chasin' things that will run:
Girls wearing perfume, tears of lilac and mum.
My mom also put that stuff behind her ears.
Those same old songs, the types that cause tears.

One Hundred Eight

❖ ❖ ❖

They started driving again. Markus was surprised by the number of curves. In Sweden the roads are straight; they lead to a destination that you can see. He let himself be lulled by the dizzy feeling, without daring to ask Natalie where they were going. Did it really matter? It was far from original to say, but he was ready to follow her to the end of the world. Did she at least know where they were headed? Maybe she just wanted to tear into the night. Race into forgetfulness.

Finally she stopped. This time in front of a small iron fence. Was this the theme of their wandering? Variations on iron fences. She got out to open the gate, then climbed back into the car. In Markus's mind, every action seemed important, stood out as something in and of itself, because that's the way you live the details of a personal mythology. The car sped up a narrow path and stopped in front of a house.

"We're at Madeleine's, my grandmother's, place. She's been living alone since my grandfather died."

"Okay. I'd like to meet her," Markus answered politely.

Natalie knocked on the door, once, twice, then a little

harder. Still nothing. "She's a bit deaf. It's better to walk around. She must be in the living room, and we'll be able to see through the window."

To get around the house, you had to take a path that had turned completely muddy in the rain. Markus held onto Natalie. He couldn't see very much. Maybe she'd gone around the wrong side? Between the house and the foliage bristling with thorns, there was practically no room to walk. Natalie slipped, taking Markus down with her. Now they were drenched and covered with mud. There certainly had been more glorious invasions; this one was becoming laughable. Natalie announced, "The best thing is to finish this on our hands and knees."

"Sure is fun following you," said Markus.

Once they'd gotten to the other side, they saw the little granny sitting in front of her fireplace. She wasn't doing anything. The image really caught Markus by surprise. That way of being there, on hold, almost oblivious to herself. Natalie knocked on the window, and this time her grandmother heard. Her face lit up immediately, and she rushed to open the window.

"Oh, my darling . . . what are you doing here? What a lovely surprise!"

"I wanted to see you . . . and to do that you have to go round."

"Yes, I know. I'm sorry, you're not the first."

They climbed through the window and were out of the rain and mud at last.

Natalie introduced Markus to her grandmother. She ran her hand over his face, then turned to her granddaughter, saying,

"He seems nice." Markus cracked a big smile as if to say, yes, it's true, I'm nice. Madeleine went on, "I think I knew another Markus a long time ago. Or maybe his name was Paulus . . . or Charlus . . . well, something that ended in -us . . . but I don't remember very well . . ."

There was an embarrassed silence. What did she mean by "I knew"? Natalie smiled and took her grandmother tightly in her arms. Watching them, Markus could imagine Natalie as a little girl. The eighties were there, with them. After a moment, he asked, "Where can I wash my hands?"

"Oh, yes. Come with me."

Natalie took his hand covered with mud and briskly led him to the bathroom.

Yes, that was it, the little girl aspect that Markus brought out in her. That way of running. That way of living the next moment before the present one. Something unbridled. They were side by side in front of the two washbasins now. As they washed, they smiled at each other almost idiotically. There were bubbles, lots of bubbles, but they weren't the bubbles of nostalgia. Markus thought, This is the most beautiful washing up of my life.

They had to change. For Natalie, it was simple. She had some of her things in her room. Madeleine asked Markus, "Do you have a change of clothes?"

"No. We left on the spur of the moment."

"Just like that?"

"Yes, just like that, exactly."

Natalie thought both of them were happy about having used the expression "just like that." They seemed excited by the idea of an unpremeditated gesture. The grandmother told Markus to go rummage through her husband's closet. She led him to the end of the hallway and left him alone to choose what he wanted. A few minutes later, he appeared wearing a suit that was half beige and half a color that was unidentifiable. His shirt collar was so enormous that his neck looked as if it were drowning. Such an outlandish getup didn't in the slightest impede his good humor. He seemed happy about being dressed this way and even mused, I'm floating inside this, but I feel good. Natalie burst out laughing to the point of getting tears in her eyes. Tears of laughter flowed down cheeks whose tears of suffering had barely dried. Madeleine came up to him, but it seemed as though she were coming up to the suit more than the man. Behind each crease was the memory of a lifetime. For an instant she stayed near her surprise guest without moving.

One Hundred Nine

❖ ❖ ❖

Perhaps because they've experienced the war, grandmothers always have something for their granddaughters to eat when they show up in the middle of the evening with a Swede.

"I hope you haven't eaten. I made some soup."

"Oh, really? What kind?" asked Markus.

"It's Friday soup. I can't explain it to you. This is Friday, so it's Friday soup."

"It's soup without a tie," Markus concluded.

Then Natalie came up to him. "Granny, sometimes he says weird things. You mustn't worry."

"Oh, me, you know, I haven't worried since 1945. So I'm fine. Come on, sit down."

Madeleine was full of vitality. There was a real discrepancy between the energy she displayed preparing dinner and the initial sight of that old woman sitting in front of the fire. This visit was giving her an enthusiasm for movement. She was busy in the kitchen, definitely not wanting any help. Natalie and Markus were disarmed by this little lady's excitement. Everything seemed so far away now: Paris, the firm, the files. Time as well was slipping away: the beginning of the afternoon at the office was a black-and-white memory. Only the name of the soup—"Friday"—still rooted them to a small extent in the concrete reality of their days.

Dinner went by easily. In silence. With grandparents, the rapt happiness of seeing their grandchildren definitely needs no spiels. You wonder if things are going all right, and very quickly you relax into the simple pleasure of being together. After dinner, Natalie helped her grandmother do the dishes. She wondered, Why did I forget how pleasant it is to be here? It was as if all the happiness she'd enjoyed had been suddenly sentenced to amnesia. She knew that she had the strength to hold onto it now.

Markus was smoking a cigar in the living room. He may have barely been able to stand cigarettes, but he wanted to please Madeleine. "She loves men to smoke a cigar after the meal. Don't try to understand. You're pleasing her, that's all," Natalie had whispered at the moment when Markus had to answer an invitation to blow smoke rings. So he expressed a strong desire for a cigar, overplaying his enthusiasm rather artlessly; but Madeleine fell for his smoke-and-mirrors act. Thus, Markus played at being the boss in a Norman household. One thing surprised him: he didn't have a headache. Worse, he was beginning to appreciate the taste of the cigar. Virility took its place inside him, hardly surprised at being there. He was experiencing that paradoxical feeling of taking life not by the horns but by hot air. With this cigar, he was Markus the Magnificent.

———

Madeleine was happy to see her granddaughter smiling. Natalie had wept so much when François died; not a single day went by without her thinking about it. Madeleine had seen a lot of tragedy in her life, but this one had been the worst. She knew you had to go forward, that life was principally about going on living. So this moment offered her profound relief. In order not to spoil anything, she felt a genuine instinctive sympathy for this Swede.

"He's a good person at heart."

"Oh, really, how can you see that?"

"I sense it. Instinct. Down deep he's fantastic."

Natalie kissed her grandmother again. It was time to go to bed. Markus put out his cigar as he said to Madeleine, "Sleep is a path that leads to tomorrow's soup."

Madeleine slept on the first floor, because climbing the stairs had become hard for her. The other bedrooms were on the floor above. Natalie looked at Markus. "She can't disturb us, the way it is." The sentence could have meant anything, could have been a sexual reference or a simple pragmatic fact, meaning, tomorrow morning we can sleep peacefully. Markus didn't want to think about it. Was he going to sleep with her: yes or no? Certainly he wanted to, but he understood they had to climb the stairs without even thinking about it. Once he was up there, he was struck again by the narrowness. After the path the car had taken, then the second path around the house, here was a third time in which he felt cramped. In that strange hallway, there were several doors, as many as there were rooms. Natalie went back and forth, without saying anything. There wasn't any electricity on this floor. She lit two candles that were on a small table. Her face was orange, but more of a sunrise orange than the sunset kind. She was hesitating, too, really hesitating. She knew that it was up to her to take the initiative. She looked at the fire, right in the eye. Then she opened the door.

One Hundred Ten

❖ ❖ ❖

Charles closed the door. He was spaced out, and might as well have been in outer space because of the great distance he felt from his body. His face hurt from being punched that day. He was perfectly aware that he'd been shabby, and that he was putting his head on the block if it got to high places in Sweden that he'd wanted to transfer an employee for personal advantage. But really, there was very little chance that anyone would know. He was certain he'd never see them again. Their running away felt definitive. And that was really what hurt him more than anything. Never to see Natalie again. It was all his fault. What he'd done was insane, and he blamed himself horribly. He just wanted to see her for a second, try to be forgiven, try to stop seeming pathetic. He wanted to find the words he'd tried so hard to find. To live in a world where there was still a chance to win her affection, a world of emotional amnesia where he could meet her again for the first time.

Now he was going into his living room. And found himself in front of an ineradicable sight: his wife on the couch. This evening scene was a museum with a single painting.

"You okay?" he murmured.

"Yes, I am. What about you?"

"You weren't worried?"

"Why?"

"Well, because of that night."

"Um, no . . . what happened that night?"

Laurence had barely turned her head. Charles had spoken to the back of his wife's neck. He'd just understood that she hadn't even noticed his absence the night before. That there was no difference between him and empty space. It was unfathomable. He wanted to hit her: balance the account for the attacks of that day, give her at least one of the slaps he'd received; but his hand stopped midway for a moment. He began to study it. There it was, his hand, in midair, forsaken. Suddenly he understood that he couldn't stand not having love anymore, that he was suffocating by living in a desiccated world. No one took him in her arms, no one showed the slightest sign of affection when it came to him. Why was it that way? He'd forgotten the existence of kindness. He was excluded from sensitivity, from delicacy.

His hand moved down again slowly, and he placed it on his wife's hair. He felt moved, truly moved, without really knowing why such an emotion was rising in him like this. He told himself that his wife had beautiful hair. Maybe that was it. He moved his hand further down, to touch the back of her neck. Certain ducts on his skin absorbed the vestige of past kisses. Memories of his ardor. He wanted to make the back of his wife's neck the point of departure for the entire reconquest of her body. He walked around the couch until he was in front of her. He fell to his knees and tried to kiss her.

"What are you doing?" she asked in a thick voice.

"I want you."

"Now?"

"Yes, now."

"You're catching me off guard."

"Come on. I've got to ask for an appointment in order to kiss you?"

"No . . . don't be stupid."

"And you know what would be great also?"

"No?"

"For us to go to Venice. Yes, I'm going to organize it . . . we'll go away for the weekend . . . the two of us . . . it'll do us some good . . ."

" . . . You know that I get seasick."

"So? That isn't serious . . . We'll go to Venice by plane."

"I'm talking about the gondolas. It's no good if you can't do the gondolas. Don't you think?"

One Hundred Eleven

❊ ❊ ❊

Thought of a Second Polish Philosopher

Only candles know the secret of dying slowly.

One Hundred Twelve

❖ ❖ ❖

Natalie entered the room where she was used to sleeping. She moved forward by the light of the candles but would very well have been able to make her way through the dark because of how well she knew the slightest nook or cranny in this room. She guided Markus, who was following her, holding her by the hips. It was the most radiant darkness of his life. He was afraid that his joy would become so intense that he'd lose all of his know-how. It's not unusual for an excess of excitement to incapacitate. He mustn't think about it, must just let himself be carried along by each second. Each breath of air a world. Natalie placed the candles on the bedside table. They met each other face to face in the poignant motion of the shadows.

She put her head on his shoulder, he caressed her hair. They could have stayed that way. It was like sleeping standing up. But he was so cold. It was also the cold of absence; no one came here anymore. It was like a place that needed to be reconquered, where memory needed to be added to memory. They lay down under the covers. Markus kept caressing Natalie's hair untiringly. He loved it so much, he wanted to know it strand by strand, understand the history and thought of each. He wanted to take a voyage in her hair. It was his sensitivity, his care not to rush the situation that made Natalie feel good. Even so, he was proactive. Currently he was undressing her, and his heart was beating with a strange force.

She was naked now, pressed against him. The emotions he felt were so powerful that his movements slowed. A slowness that almost took the form of a retreat. He was letting immense apprehension eat away at him, was beginning to muddle it. She loved these moments when he was clumsy, when he hesitated. She understood that she'd wanted that more than anything, to rediscover men through a man who was not at all a frequenter of women. So that together they could rediscover the handbook of affection. There was something restful about being with him. Perhaps it was arrogant or shallow to say so, but it seemed to her that this man would always be happy to be with her. She had the feeling that their relationship as a couple would enjoy extreme stability. That nothing could happen. That their physical equation was an antidote to death. All of it she thought in snatches, without being very certain. She only knew that this was the moment, and that in such situations it's always the body that decides. He was on top of her now. She clung to him tightly.

Tears ran down her temples. He kissed her tears.

And from her tears others were born as well; his, this time.

One Hundred Thirteen

❖   ❖   ❖

Beginning of Chapter 7 of Hopscotch
by Julio Cortázar,
the Book Natalie Was Reading
at the Beginning of This Novel

"I touch your mouth, I touch the edge of your mouth with my finger, I am drawing it as if it were something my hand was sketching, as if for the first time your mouth opened a little, and all I have to do is close my eyes to erase it and start all over again, every time I can make the mouth I want appear, the mouth which my hand chooses and sketches on your face, and which by some chance that I do not seek to understand coincides exactly with your mouth which smiles beneath the one my hand is sketching on you."*

---

* Translator's note: from *Hopscotch* (original Spanish title: *Rayuela*), translated from the Spanish by Gregory Rabassa. Copyright © 1966 by Random House.

One Hundred Fourteen

❖ ❖ ❖

Early morning had come already. It was as if the night had never existed. Natalie and Markus had alternated between moments of wakefulness and dozing, blurring in that way the frontiers between dream and reality.

"I'd really like to go down to the garden," said Natalie.

"Now?"

"Yes, you'll see. When I was little, I always went there in the morning. There's a strange atmosphere at dawn."

They got up quickly and dressed slowly.* Looking at each other, discovering each other in the cold light. It was simple. They came down the stairs without making any noise, in order not to wake Madeleine. A needless precaution, since she barely slept when she had guests. But she wasn't going to disturb them. She knew Natalie's penchant for the calm of mornings in the garden (to each her own ritual). In all weathers, every time that she came here, she went to sit on the bench as soon as she opened her eyes. They were outdoors. Natalie stopped to

---

* It may have been the opposite.

observe each detail. Life could go on, life could destroy, but here nothing budged: the sphere of the unchanging.

They sat down. There was genuine wonder between them, that of physical pleasure. Something that had to do with the magic of tales, instants flown to perfection. Minutes that you burn into your memory at the very moment you are living them. Seconds that are our future nostalgia. "I feel good," whispered Natalie, and Markus was truly happy. She got up. He watched her walking to the flowers and trees. She made several slow back-and-forth trips, gently musing, letting her hand touch everything that happened to be in reach. Here her relationship with nature was deeply intimate. Then she stopped. Right against a tree.

"When I used to play hide-and-seek with my cousins, you were supposed to stand against this tree to count. It went on for a long time. We'd count to 117."

"Why 117?"

"I don't know! We just decided on that figure, like that."

"Do you want to play now?" offered Markus.

Natalie smiled at him. She adored his being able to offer to play. She took her position against the tree, closed her eyes, and began to count. Markus went off in search of a good place to hide. A futile ambition: this was Natalie's domain. She had to know the best places. As he looked around, he thought of all those places where she'd already have to have hidden. He was walking through Natalie's ages. At seven, she must have gone under that tree. At twelve, she had to have burrowed into this bush. As a teenager, she'd rejected childhood games and had

gone on past those brambles, sulking. And the following summer, it was as a young woman that she'd sat on this bench, a
daydreaming poet, her heart filled with the hope of romance.
Her life as a young woman had left its traces in several places,
and might she even have made love behind these flowers? François had run behind her, trying to tear off her nightie, without
making too much noise, to keep from waking her grandparents,
traces of a reckless and silent dash across the garden. And then
he'd caught her. She'd tried to struggle, without seeming very
believable. She'd turned her head, while dreaming of his kisses.
They'd rolled along, and then she'd ended up alone. Where was
he? Was he hiding somewhere? He wasn't there anymore. He'd
never be there. At that place, there was no more grass. Natalie
had torn it all out in rage. Here is where she'd lie flat on the
ground for hours, and her grandmother's attempts to make her
come back inside hadn't changed anything. By walking to that
very spot, Markus was treading on her suffering. He was going
through the tears of her love. As he kept looking for his hiding
place, he also walked over all the places where Natalie would go
later. Now and then, he was moved by imagining the old woman
she'd be.

Thus, at the heart of all the Natalies, Markus found a place to
hide. He made himself as small as possible. A strange thing to
do on this day on which he felt bigger than ever. Throughout his
entire body, impulses of immensity awoke. Once they were in
place, he began to smile. He was happy to wait for her, so happy
to wait for her to discover him.

One Hundred Fifteen

Natalie opened her eyes.

THE END